NO

Powerful searchlights suddenly flooded the factory with blinding white light. Unable to see for a minute, the Hardys froze. Then they heard a metal door slide shut with an ominous clang.

Shading his eyes with his hands, Joe peered out and saw that the only exit was blocked by a locked metal gate. Then his attention was caught by Whip Scorpion's shiny form as he stepped out of the darkness into the light.

Whip Scorpion flicked his bullwhip with a sharp pop and brandished a ninja star in his other hand. Joe turned again as Flame Fiend appeared on the other side of them, shooting a burst of fire from his hand.

"Now we settle accounts," a gravelly voice announced from behind the boys.

Frank knew that voice. It belonged to the Human Dreadnought. The Hardys were surrounded.

Books in THE HARDY BOYS CASEFILES® Series

#1 DEAD ON TARGET
#2 EVIL, INC.
#3 CULT OF CRIME
#4 THE LAZARUS PLOT
#5 EDGE OF DESTRUCTION
#6 THE CROWNING TERROR
#7 DEATHGAME
#8 SEE NO EVIL
#9 THE GENIUS THIEVES
#10 HOSTAGES OF HATE
#11 BROTHER AGAINST BROTHER
#12 PERFECT GETAWAY
#13 THE BORGIA DAGGER
#14 TOO MANY TRAITORS
#15 BLOOD RELATIONS
#16 LINE OF FIRE
#17 THE NUMBER FILE
#18 A KILLING IN THE MARKET
#19 NIGHTMARE IN ANGEL CITY
#20 WITNESS TO MURDER
#21 STREET SPIES
#22 DOUBLE EXPOSURE
#23 DISASTER FOR HIRE
#24 SCENE OF THE CRIME
#25 THE BORDERLINE CASE
#26 TROUBLE IN THE PIPELINE
#27 NOWHERE TO RUN
#28 COUNTDOWN TO TERROR
#29 THICK AS THIEVES
#30 THE DEADLIEST DARE
#31 WITHOUT A TRACE
#32 BLOOD MONEY
#33 COLLISION COURSE
#34 FINAL CUT
#35 THE DEAD SEASON
#36 RUNNING ON EMPTY
#37 DANGER ZONE
#38 DIPLOMATIC DECEIT
#39 FLESH AND BLOOD
#40 FRIGHT WAVE
#41 HIGHWAY ROBBERY
#42 THE LAST LAUGH

Available from ARCHWAY Paperbacks

	DATE DUE		
FEB 18 1991			
MAR 5 1991	AUG. 12 1992	MR 24 '05	
MAR. 20 1991	SEP 9 1992	MY 26 '09	
APR. 5 1991	FEB 27 1993	JE 09 '11	
MAY 6 1991			
MAY 28 1991	AUG 30 1994		
JUL 3 1991			
JUL 29 1991	AUG 17 '95		
AUG 13 1991	JUL 23 1996		
OCT 17 1991	JA 12 '98		
JAN 13 1992	AG 25 '04		

Dixon, Franklin W.
The last laugh
Hardy Boys Casefiles #42

This book is a work of fiction. Names, characters, places and incidents are either the product of the author's imagination or are used fictitiously. Any resemblance to actual events or locales or persons, living or dead, is entirely coincidental.

An ARCHWAY PAPERBACK *Original*

An Archway Paperback published by
POCKET BOOKS, a division of Simon & Schuster Inc.
1230 Avenue of the Americas, New York, NY 10020

Produced by Mega-Books of New York, Inc.

ISBN: 0-671-70039-1

First Archway Paperback printing August 1990

10 9 8 7 6 5 4 3 2 1

Printed in the U.S.A.

IL 7+

Chapter 1

"I STILL SAY comic books are kid stuff," Joe Hardy insisted, brushing a lock of blond hair off his forehead. "Why go to a comic-book convention when the beaches and girls of sunny San Diego are calling?"

Joe stopped on the sidewalk and held his arms straight out, making his brother, Frank, and their friend Chet Morton stop, too.

Frank Hardy turned his brother around to face him. At eighteen, Frank was a year older than Joe and had darker coloring—brown hair and eyes. He was an inch taller than his younger brother and slimmer, although both boys had strong, athletic builds.

"Joe, we all agreed to go to the convention first," Frank said firmly. "Besides, why don't you broaden your horizons? There'll be plenty of time to hit the beach when the convention's over. We have a week before we have to head east, back to Bayport."

"Yeah, don't be so quick to knock it, Joe," Chet Morgan put in, his round face serious.

Joe wanted to smile at Chet because of the way he dressed, but he held back. Chet was wearing a T-shirt with the Green Cyclone lifting a skyscraper, baggy khaki pants that flapped in the breeze, and canvas high-top sneakers covered with the laughing face of an insane comic character that Joe didn't recognize.

"Conventions are a blast. There's always tons of stuff to do and see. Original artwork going back to the forties is on display during the whole con. Tomorrow night there's that big costume contest, and the night after that, the convention dance."

"Anyway, Joe, if you want to meet California girls, why don't you just turn around?" Frank insisted.

Joe turned in time to see a group of girls dressed in shorts and superhero T-shirts pass by, laughing and talking excitedly.

Joe's face brightened at the sight, and he fell into step behind the girls, saying, "Hmmm, this might be worth checking out after all."

Frank and Chet exchanged knowing glances and shook their heads.

"Come on, guys," Joe called. "The con awaits."

As Frank and Chet hurried to catch up to him, Joe turned to Frank and said, "Maybe you could keep up better if you weren't weighed down with all the junk you carry in that shoulder bag."

"Junk!" Frank answered scornfully. "You didn't think it was junk when you wanted to borrow my camera this morning. Besides, you never know when something might come up—like a case."

The Hardys' father, Fenton Hardy, was a famous private investigator, and the boys were also well-known as investigators.

"Hey, guys, stop arguing and hurry or we'll miss Barry Johns's talk," Chet said.

"Who's Barry Johns?" Joe asked.

Chet filled the Hardys in as they lined up to buy their convention memberships. Although it was only one o'clock, the line for memberships already stretched out the entrance of the convention center and past the fountain that dominated the convention-center plaza.

"Johns helped organize some of the very first comic cons back in the early sixties," Chet explained. "He was also one of the first fans to break into the comics business."

"Is that unusual?" Frank asked.

"Not these days," Chet said. "But back then most people got into comics by writing for the pulp magazines, or by working as assistants for established cartoonists."

Joe was restlessly shifting his weight from one foot to the other as they waited. "What are pulp magazines?" he asked, his eyes darting back and forth, checking out the girls.

"They're what people used to read before they had paperbacks. Pulps were little magazines full of short stories. They had titles like *Weird Tales* and *Nickel Western*. They were printed on the cheapest paper available," Chet answered. "That's how they got their name—pulp magazines."

Joe nodded distractedly, not really listening. Frank and Chet continued to talk while Joe continued to look around.

"This line is hardly moving," he muttered to no one in particular. "There must be a bottleneck in the lobby."

Chet's round face lit up. "That must be where they've set up Barry Johns's collection of comic-book artwork. This is going to be great!" he said.

"What's so great about a bunch of old comic-book pages?" Joe asked.

"Joe, you don't understand. Johns has one of the best collections of comic art in the country. I heard it's insured for about a million dollars."

Frank and Joe both raised their eyebrows in surprise.

Joe emitted a low whistle. "A million bucks, huh? I had no idea the stuff was worth so much."

"Why is this art collection so valuable?" Frank asked.

"Because most of it's from the Golden Age—" Chet began.

"Hey, the line's moving," Joe cut in. The boys began walking toward the convention center's open double doors again.

"The Golden Age is the period from the late thirties until the midforties," Chet continued. "Stuff from that time's really valuable because of the high quality of some of the drawings and because not much has survived."

"Why is that?" Frank inquired.

"Until the early sixties not many people realized comic-book art had any artistic value, so nobody bothered to save it except for a few artists who kept work that they liked."

By this time they had reached the convention-center doors and filed through. In the lobby the boys were directed to the registration table. Chet suggested that they all buy memberships for the entire convention. They were given plastic membership badges, program books, and small plastic shopping bags filled with fliers, brochures, and promotional buttons.

Joe briefly flipped through his con package, then checked out the lobby. Lots of people were milling around, and the babble of excited voices was constantly punctuated by bursts of laughter. Against the far wall of the lobby Joe spotted a large group of people gathered around double-sided display stands. He moved closer and saw a placard on the wall that explained the stands held Barry Johns's collection of artwork.

People began filing into the convention center's main auditorium, and the crowd around the Plexiglas-covered pages of yellowing illustration board shrank to a few.

Frank and Chet joined Joe at the display as a loudspeaker announced that Barry Johns would be making his keynote address in five minutes.

Frank started toward the auditorium entrance, but Chet laid a restraining hand on his arm.

"Wait, Frank. Let's check out the artwork before Johns's speech."

"But I though you wanted to hear this guy talk," Joe said.

"I do," Chet told him. "I just wanted to see his collection without too many people around. We can give it a quick look now and slip in before Johns starts his speech."

"Suits me," said Joe with a shrug. "I'm curious to see this stuff after hearing how much it's worth."

The display was totally deserted now. A big smile slowly spread across Chet's face as he stared intently at a comic-book cover from 1942 that depicted a muscular, square-jawed hero in a star-spangled costume slugging Adolf Hitler.

Peering over Frank's shoulder, Joe saw that his brother was studying some pages with an army of Amazon women in metal breastplates and short skirts battling a horde of lizardlike aliens.

Joe moved on, glancing briefly at several pages, but nothing held his attention until he came to a large cover illustration from a comic called *Wonder Tales*. The cover was of a giant blond strongman fighting an equally huge robot in the middle of Manhattan. A second robot in the background was climbing over a landscape of wrecked skyscrapers. Joe smiled at the clunky, old-fashioned robots, but he liked the cover as a piece of art. The lines of the hero's figure were as slick and well-drawn as any illustration he'd ever seen, and the colors were sharp and vibrant.

"Come on, you guys. We'd better go," Chet said, signaling the Hardys.

Chet led the way to a side door into the main auditorium. The hall seated several thousand people, and it was packed. Fans were standing along the back and side walls. Joe scanned the room, looking for any place to squeeze in.

"There's nowhere to sit or even stand," he

complained. "I knew I should have gone to the beach."

Joe turned at the sound of a loud whisper from their right, near the front of the hall.

"*Psst*, Chet! Hey, Chet!"

A tall red-haired teenager with round wire-framed glasses was waving them to come over. Chet obviously recognized the boy and waved back. He and the Hardys carefully picked their way down the crowded aisle to join the boy leaning against the wall. He smiled broadly as he pumped Chet's hand.

"Hi, Chet. Good to see you, buddy," he whispered.

"Same here," said Chet. "Tom, meet some friends of mine, Frank and Joe Hardy." He turned to the Hardys. "Tom lives in San Diego. We always get together at cons."

Joe and Frank leaned around Chet to shake the redhead's hand.

"Hi, fellas. I'm Tom Gatlin."

"Nice to meet you, Tom," Frank replied.

"Chet's told me a lot about you guys."

"Some of it good, I hope," Joe cracked.

Just then the lights went down, and a pleasant-looking blond woman walked across the stage to the speaker's platform.

Chet leaned over to whisper to the Hardys. "That's Sandy Mendoza, the president of the con."

"Good afternoon, everybody," said the

woman, "and welcome to the Twenty-first Annual San Diego Comic Convention. It's my pleasure to introduce the convention's guest of honor, Barry Johns, president of Zenith Publishing."

Loud applause broke out. Johns strode to the speaker's podium, smiling and waving. He was a moon-faced, boyish-looking man in his late thirties with clear brown eyes behind his tortoiseshell glasses. He was dressed in an expensive gray suit.

Johns raised a hand to silence the crowd, then began speaking. "Hi, folks. It's great to be back at the San Diego Con again. But then, it's always great to be here."

The crowd erupted in loud cheering, forcing Johns to motion for silence again.

"Johns seems very popular," Frank commented.

"He is," Chet told him. "He's got one of the most successful new comic-book companies in the country. He writes and draws two comics a month, and writes a couple of others, too. He does *Metaman*."

"*Metaman?*" Joe asked in a puzzled voice. "Never heard of it."

"That's because you don't read comics," Chet responded. "It's only one of the best-selling comics in the country."

"*Shh.*" Tom Gatlin elbowed Chet. "Can you talk later? I want to hear this."

Up on the stage, Johns was speaking in a pleasant, slightly high-pitched voice.

"And a lot of fans have asked how I broke into the business. Well, it wasn't easy. It took me a couple of years of writing and calling all the major comics companies before I could even get in the door to show them my samples. I worked hard to make my own drawing and writing better. Studying the work of the best cartoonists and illustrators . . ."

John's voice trailed off as the doors closest to the stage swung open and two costumed figures burst into the auditorium. The larger of the two led the way, roughly pushing audience members aside. The man's massive frame was encased in what looked to Joe like blue-gray metal armor that included a breastplate, shin guards, and forearm guards that ended at metal-studded gloves. His breastplate was criss-crossed with bandoliers holding a dozen grenades. The square helmet he wore had a smooth silver visor that completely concealed his face.

The second figure wore a tight red-and-black costume with red tights. His head, except for the lower half of his face, was encased in a tight black hood with a flamelike splash of red across the nose and eyes.

As the two men approached the stage the crowed began cheering and applauding.

"That's the Human Dreadnought and Flame Fiend," Chet whispered excitedly. "They're supervillains from Terrific Comics. Terrific Comics is one of Johns's biggest rivals. I bet this is some kind of publicity stunt."

The crowd's cheering quickly stopped after the Human Dreadnought grabbed a convention security guard and threw him against a wall. Flame Fiend slugged another security guard in the jaw, sending him reeling. Then he leapt up onto the stage. Barry Johns was frozen in place, his hands tightly gripping the sides of the speaker's podium.

Joe watched, horrified. This didn't look like any publicity stunt to him. He started to take a step in the direction of the stage, when the Human Dreadnought pulled the pins from two grenades and hurled them into the aisles. The grenades didn't explode but began spewing clouds of jet-black smoke. Joe heard some coughing, and as the smoke spread, someone in the crowd started screaming.

All at once everyone began rushing for the exits. Joe felt the press of panic-stricken people wedge him against the wall. He couldn't budge.

They're going to trample me, Joe thought.

Chapter 2

JOE PEERED THROUGH the smoke at Frank. "How are we going to get out of here?" he yelled, but Frank couldn't hear him or see him.

"This is no publicity stunt, Chet!" Frank shouted into his friend's ear. As the smoke was disappearing, Frank saw the Human Dreadnought toss four more smoke grenades into the aisles, causing even greater panic. People were coughing and screaming and shoving their way to the exits to escape the choking clouds of smoke. The smoke alarms suddenly sounded, adding to the growing confusion.

Frank, who had pushed his way into a row where the smoke was much less dense, saw Flame Fiend grab Sandy Mendoza and push her off the front of the stage. Then Frank could just make out Flame Fiend turning on Johns, who had let go of the podium and was backing away from him.

Frank covered his nose and mouth with one hand and tried to move toward the stage, straining to see what was happening up there. Through the tears that were clouding his vision, Frank watched the Human Dreadnought leap up onto the stage. Johns dodged behind the chairs that had been set up on the stage, but the Dreadnought tossed them aside with one sweep of his arm. He crossed the space between himself and Johns with one leap. Johns put his fists up and backed up to the rear wall.

"Looks like a pretty unfair fight," he heard Joe call out from quite nearby. "What say we even the odds a little?"

"You read my mind, Joe," Frank shouted. "Better stay put, Chet!"

"Can't do much else right now!" Chet called from his spot against the wall, where the crowd still had him pinned.

Frank jumped onto the arms of a chair, and Joe followed his lead. Leaping from row to row, the Hardys made good speed toward the front of the auditorium.

As they reached the first row of chairs, Frank watched the Dreadnought punch Johns in the stomach, doubling him over. Then before Frank could vault onto the stage, the armored giant had picked up Johns and slung him over his shoulder. The Dreadnought ran for the nearest door, pulling another smoke grenade off his belt and tossing it over his shoulder. Flame Fiend followed close behind his friend, turning to check for pursuers.

The Hardys scrambled onto the stage and charged after the two comic-book figures, coughing as the acrid smoke entered their lungs. Despite the smoke, Joe managed to catch a glimpse of Flame Fiend as he disappeared through the double doors.

"Frank! They went this way!" Joe called. He grabbed Frank and pulled him toward the doors. The Hardys hit the doors as hard as they could, but they held fast.

"They blocked them from the other side!" Frank shouted. "Let's try again."

Frank and Joe hurled themselves against the doors again. This time they heard a cracking noise, and the doors gave slightly. Joe reared back for another try, but Frank stopped him as Chet stumbled onto the stage coughing and waving a hand to disperse the smoke.

"Those guys blocked off these doors, Chet," Joe told him. "We need to hit them one more time."

"I'm your man," Chet replied firmly. "Let's do it, guys."

The trio threw themselves at the doors, and this time they gave way with a splintering crash. A mop handle that had been rammed through the handles fell to the floor in two pieces.

As the boys raced into the hall, Frank saw that the Dreadnought, with Johns slung over his shoulder, had reached the lobby and was heading for a door opening onto the convention-center plaza. The Dreadnought turned just then and pulled off another smoke bomb. He lobbed it to Flame Fiend and bolted through the open doors and across the plaza. To Frank's surprise, Flame Fiend set the smoke bomb in the center of the lobby without pulling the pin. As he sped forward, Frank watched as Flame Fiend strode over to Johns's collection of comics. With a theatrical flourish, Flame Fiend snapped his fingers. A flame appeared in his palm. Frank stopped short, watching in disbelief as the flame grew into a foot-long wand of fire. Flame Fiend walked along the rows of Plexiglas-covered comic-book art, spraying fire over each display stand. This is too much, thought Frank. It's like something out of a comic book, but it's really happening!

"He's burning the whole collection!" Chet shouted. "We've got to stop him!"

Joe charged across the lobby toward the red-and-black figure with Frank. Chet puffed along, bringing up the rear.

"Hey!" Joe shouted, running straight at Flame Fiend as the last of the display stands was sprayed with fire.

Flame Fiend whirled at the shout and faced the boys. He snapped his fingers again, and the column of flame in his left hand vanished. Then with a peal of crazy laughter he kicked over the nearest display stand so it knocked over the stand next to it. The stands cascaded toward the Hardys like a row of flaming dominoes. Joe skidded to a stop, but he and Frank were directly in the path of the tumbling, flaming stands.

Just in time, Frank dived to the left and Joe rolled to the right. The blazing Plexiglas-and-wood frames toppled in a heap, flames separating the Hardys.

Frank pulled himself up, looking over the flames for Joe, who was already disappearing through the lobby doors. Shaking his head, Frank grabbed a fire extinguisher from a nearby pillar and began to put out the fire.

Arms and legs pumping furiously, Joe sprinted across the broad plaza. Flame Fiend had a good lead, but Joe was faster and was gaining on him.

Joe saw the crook glance behind him. Then Flame Fiend's left hand flipped open a small black box on the back of his belt. A second later Joe heard a rapid metallic clattering.

Before Joe knew what was happening, he lost his footing and felt his feet shoot up in the air. He slammed into the ground, hard.

The fall knocked the wind from his lungs, and Joe just lay there for a moment. He shook his head to clear it, and when his eyes focused, he caught a flash of movement near the corner of the parking garage. It was Flame Fiend, climbing into a silver van with tinted gray windows. The van roared off as Joe watched in angry frustration.

Fuming, Joe glanced around him and spotted a shiny metal ball lodged in a groove in the pavement. Then he noticed several others.

"Ball bearings," Joe muttered, plucking one of the metal balls from the pavement.

He examined the ball bearings to see if it could give any clue to its origins, but it was featureless. He almost threw it down in disgust. But then he remembered his father's advice that no clue was too small for a good detective. Joe pocketed the ball bearing, got to his feet, and walked briskly back to the lobby.

Frank was standing near the burned pile of display stands, holding a fire extinguisher, when Joe got there. Frank barely noticed Joe's arrival. The stands were no longer burning, Joe saw, but the artwork they'd displayed was reduced to ashes. The room was still smoky, and people had begun to open doors on either end of the lobby to air the space out. A handful of people wearing convention badges milled about, talking excitedly.

"What happened?" Frank asked as Joe joined him.

"They got away. I almost had the one in the red-and-black long johns, but he dropped a bunch of ball bearings and I slipped on them."

"Cute." Frank grimaced.

"I saved one," Joe went on, "and I got a look at the getaway vehicle."

Frank's expression brightened. "Good going. What was it?"

"A silver van, one of those new ones with a real sleek aerodynamic design. It had a gray-tinted wraparound windshield, so I couldn't see inside."

"Did you get the license number?" Frank asked.

"Nope." Joe shook his head. "The van pulled out too fast."

Using a handkerchief, Frank held up a smoke bomb. "I picked up one of these as evidence," he told Joe. "I hope it'll tell us more about the kidnappers than your ball bearing."

"Is that the smoke bomb Flame Fiend set down in the lobby?" Joe asked.

"Yes." The look on Frank's face grew thoughtful. "Didn't it seem odd that he set that one smoke bomb down so carefully when Dreadnought just flung the others around?"

Joe nodded. "Yeah, I thought so, too."

A sudden babble of voices caused Frank to look up at a small crowd of people that had gathered near them to stare at the smoking ashes of Barry Johns's collection of comic-book artwork. Frank had already moved away when he noticed Chet's friend Tom Gatlin. Gatlin seemed nervous and was looking around furtively. Suddenly he slipped through the crowd and out of sight.

Frowning, Frank absently rolled the smoke bomb around in his hand. He was about to mention Gatlin's behavior to Joe when an idea struck him.

"Hey, this bomb feels too light," he said, shaking it beside his ear. He heard a rustling sound.

Chet walked up then and eyed him nervously. "Take it easy with that thing," he warned. "It might go off."

"The pin's still in it, Chet," Frank replied as he turned the smoke bomb over to examine the bottom.

Then, as Chet watched uncertainly, Frank grabbed the top of the grenade and began to unscrew it.

"Are you crazy!" Chet exclaimed, but Frank paid no attention. As he suspected, the bomb was hollow. Inside was a small envelope made of metallic silver paper. Frank opened his handkerchief and carefully shook the envelope into it. Touching the metallic paper only with a handkerchief, Frank opened it and withdrew a small square of white paper. Then he set the envelope down beside the hollow grenade and carefully unfolded the paper.

"What's it say, Frank?" Joe asked impatiently.

Frank read silently, then handed the note to Joe with a grim expression.

In neat computer printout type, the note read:

> Mrs. Barry Johns,
>
> You will give us $500,000 in two days, or your husband's a dead man. We mean business. Ransom-delivery instructions to follow.
>
> The Human Dreadnought

Chapter

3

JOE HARDY STARED in disbelief at the note in his hand. "This has got to be the weirdest kidnapping I ever heard of.

"It's real, though, unfortunately," Frank said.

Taking the ransom note back from Joe, he set it and the metallic-paper envelope on the caeted floor. He fished around in his shoulder bag and drew out a small black leatherbound notebook and pen. Frank copied the ransom message in the notebook, making notes about the appearance of the envelope and notepaper.

The wail of approaching sirens cut through the air. Glancing through the glass-and-chrome doors at the front of the lobby, Joe saw two black-and-white police cars and a couple of red fire trucks rumbling toward the convention center. Soon some San Diego cops were shooing people out of the way of the firemen, who rushed in carrying big-tank fire extinguishers. They relaxed when they realized that, despite all the smoke, the fire was out.

A tall cop with a thin mustache quickly took charge. Frank stowed his notebook, picked up the dummy grenade and ransom note, and walked over to the cop.

"Officer, there's just been a kidnapping!"

"What?" The cop regarded Frank dubiously through dark aviator shades. "We got a call only about a possible fire here. Who got kidnapped?"

Joe stepped up beside his brother. "It was Barry Johns, the guest of honor at this convention," he told the cop.

"I think this is a ransom note for Johns," Frank added. He held out the note and fake smoke bomb to the tall police officer, whose badge said Leinster.

The cop looked annoyed. "You shouldn't disturb evidence. What's your name, kid?"

"Frank Hardy, officer. Look, I can explain why I picked it up. It seemed to be one of the smoke grenades the kidnappers used. I just wanted to get it outside before it went off. But when I picked it up, it felt too light, so I opened it and found this note. But don't worry, I didn't smudge the prints," Frank explained.

Another cop walked up with quick strides. He was a short, very muscular Hispanic officer. Whipping out his own handkerchief, he took the grenade, ransom note, and envelope.

"Hold that stuff for the FBI guys, Mario," Leinster told the other officer.

"Did you get a look at the kidnappers, Mr. Hardy?" Leinster asked.

"I saw their van," Joe volunteered. "It was a new silver panel van with a tinted wraparound windshield."

"Did you see the plates?" Leinster asked sharply.

Joe shook his head. "Sorry. It was too far away."

"Could be that the van's still in the area," Leinster said. "From your description, I'd say it was a Futuro Five Thousand. They're new, not many on the road yet, so it ought to be easy to spot." He reached for the walkie-talkie hooked on his belt and called in the description.

Officer Leinster took down the name of the Hardys' hotel and told them he'd be in touch. As he walked toward his partner, who was standing by the double doors, a bulletin crackled over their radios. The dispatcher described a kidnapping that had just taken place and gave the address: 8311 Lake Baca Drive, the home of a Sydney Kaner. His wife had phoned in the distress call.

Chet was standing a few feet away from the Hardys, watching morosely as the firemen dug through the ashes of Johns's collection. Suddenly his eyes bulged in surprise. "Syd Kaner! He works for Barry Johns!"

Joe and Frank exchanged a startled look.

"Think there's a connection?" Joe asked.

"There's only one way to find out. Let's get over there right away!" Frank and Joe headed for the lobby door, with Chet bringing up the rear, shouting, "Wait for me, fellas!"

They sprinted along the plaza to the garage. As Joe opened the driver's-side door of their rental car, Frank opened the trunk and pulled out a radio with police and emergency bands and a San Diego road atlas. Closing the trunk, Frank dived through the front passenger door as Chet got in the back. They were still buckling their seat belts when Joe threw the car into reverse, backed out, and roared off toward the exit ramp.

"I'll navigate," Frank said, while trying to tune in the police band.

Frank had the radio locked onto the police band by the time Joe reached street level. He directed Joe to turn north on First Avenue, then east on A Street.

Joe wove expertly through the late-afternoon San Diego traffic, following Frank's directions. Within ten minutes they'd left the downtown area and were on the Ocean Beach Freeway, heading toward the suburban neighborhood where, according to their map, Lake Baca Drive was located.

"You looked so sad about Johns's art collection getting fried, someone would think it was yours, Chet," Joe said, glancing at Chet in the rearview mirror.

"I'm upset about the waste, Joe," Chet replied. "A whole collection of irreplaceable comic art, gone like that!" He snapped his fingers to punctuate the statement. "There were some real classics in there, some of the most beautiful comics covers of all time."

"I just never realized comic art was so valuable, Chet," Frank said.

"It hasn't always been worth much," Chet pointed out. "For years, and I'm talking two, three, four decades, newspaper syndicates and comic-book companies would just dump artwork in a storeroom until it was full. And then they'd toss it out or burn it."

"Then how did Johns get so much of it?" Frank inquired.

"He got a lot of it from Golden Age artists," Chet told him. "He'd find the artists and get to know them. He'd either buy the artwork for a low price, or they'd give it to him because they liked him."

"And now people pay a lot of money for this stuff?" Joe asked.

"Sure. Collectors like my friend Tom and

movie stars and rock-'n'-roll singers. You'd be surprised. But, hey, if you want a real expert's opinion, ask Tom. He knows more about comic-book art and cartoonists than anyone else I know."

Frank suddenly remembered how strangely Tom had acted right after the fire. He was about to mention it to the others, but then he saw their exit coming up. "Get off here, Joe," he said.

Soon they were traveling through the hilly streets of a pleasant suburban neighborhood. Frank spotted a couple of street signs, then buried his nose in the map again.

"Take a right at the next corner, Joe," he instructed. "Then go down two streets and hang a left. That ought to put us right on Lake Baca Drive."

Chet leaned forward between the Hardys. "I sure hope we don't run into Flame Fiend or Dreadnought again," he said with a worried expression.

"But that's exactly what we want," Frank told him. "Why are you so worried, Chet? What could we be up against?"

Chet leaned back and ticked off the points on his fingers as he spoke. "Let's see—in the comics the Human Dreadnought has superstrength, can run seventy miles an hour, and is invulnerable to anything smaller than an artillery shell."

Joe rolled his eyes. "What about the firebug in the red suit?" he asked.

"Flame Fiend? He can shoot blasts of flame or bursts of blinding light from his hands. He's impervious to fire and bullets and doesn't need to breathe."

Joe slapped the steering wheel and hooted. "Oh, come on, Chet. You can't possibly believe those guys are real?"

Chet replied with a noncommittal shrug.

When Joe turned the corner of Lake Baca Drive, all he saw was another ordinary suburban street lined with neat split-level homes. A minute later, however, he noticed a trio of police cars clustered around a split-level house at the end of the street.

There were tire tracks digging a double arc into the neatly manicured front lawn. An outdoor light had been knocked at a crazy angle, and the front door of the house had been battered in and lay on its side against the inside wall.

"Pull over, Joe," Frank directed, "but not too close to the police cars."

"What's the plan?" Joe asked.

"Just a little eavesdropping on the police band to see what they know," Frank answered.

Just then a green BMW drove slowly past the Kaner house, speeding up as soon as it passed. As the car swung by the Hardys' sedan, Joe got a quick glimpse of the driver, a dark-haired, middle-aged man with a large nose and a sharp profile.

Reports of related crimes poured in over Frank's radio. There was a burst of static; then a loud, tinny voice announced, "This is Charlie One at the intersection of Ashwood Avenue and Lake Murray Boulevard. I've got a make on a van resembling the one reported in the Syd Kaner kidnapping going northeast on Lake Murray." There was another burst of static before an answering voice came on.

"Roger, Charlie One. Pursue suspect vehicle immediately. Backup is en route, and you have eyes in the sky."

Joe heard the faint buzz of beating rotors. He stuck his head out the car window, and quickly spotted a San Diego police helicopter in the sky to the northeast.

The helicopter pilot's voice cut in on the police band. "Charlie One, this is Icarus. I have you and suspect van in sight, going northeast on Lake Murray. Your backup will rendezvous at Mono Lake Drive."

Frank studied the map. "Hey, that van's heading back toward us," he announced.

The chopper pilot's voice cut back on the radio in a crackle of static. "Hey, where'd they go? Charlie One, do you have a visual?"

"Negative," the boys heard Charlie One respond. "The van disappeared down a side street. Can you see anything?"

"No," the chopper pilot responded. "The trees are too thick. I'll circle. Pick a side street, and we'll flush them out."

"I think I know where they're going, Joe," Frank announced.

"And how do you know this when the cops just lost them?" Joe asked.

"I think they'll come out on Lake Ashmere Drive," Frank said excitedly. "On my map, Lake Ashmere intersects with a little access road that runs right out to the highway. It'd make a dandy getaway route."

Joe smiled and threw the car into reverse. "How do I get there?"

Four minutes later Joe had parked their rental car across the mouth of a narrow alley that ran parallel to a steep hill.

Chet leaned forward between the Hardys, a worried expression on his face. "I hope you guys know what you're doing."

Joe smiled. "Relax, Chet. This isn't a comic book, you know. Those crooks may have fancy costumes, but I'm willing to bet they're not immune to a punch in the jaw."

Frank continued to monitor the police band, hearing the growing frustration in the officers' voices as they tried unsuccessfully to locate the fugitive van.

He glanced over at Joe. "All we have to do is hold them up long enough for the police to get here."

"And how are we supposed to do that?" Joe asked.

Before Frank had a chance to answer, Joe saw a silver van barreling down the alley toward them.

"That's the same van that Flame Fiend loaded Johns into at the convention center!" Joe said.

The van screeched to a halt in a cloud of dust, and the door on the driver's side popped open. The Human Dreadnought jumped out, carrying a silver device with a long handle. He charged over to Joe's window and pounded on it. "Move that car, sonny, now."

"No way," Joe said firmly.

"Okay, punk, you asked for it!" the Dreadnought replied in a gravelly voice.

The Dreadnought began battering at the windshield with his fist, bringing his metal-studded gloves down again and again on the glass. The car was rocking with his pounding. Spiderweb cracks appeared in all directions, and the boys could hardly see out.

A second later they heard a scraping sound on the underside of the car, then a series of loud, ratcheting clicks. Frank could see the Dreadnought bent over at the rear passenger-side door.

Suddenly Frank felt his side of the car being lifted up.

"Hey—he's picking the car up!" Chet shouted.

The boys grabbed at the door handles for support as the car landed on its left side, wobbled in that position for a few seconds, then rolled over onto the roof and rocked from side to side with the boys suspended upside down.

With the blood rushing to his head, Joe could hear another scraping of metal on metal. Then the ratcheting clicks began again, and the car fell on its right side and then onto the wheels. Joe had only a moment to brace himself before the car began its dizzying roll once again. It kept rolling over and over, down the steep hillside, steadily picking up speed.

Chapter 4

THIS IS IT, Frank thought, reaching out to steady himself against the jolting of the car. He was ready for the car to burst into flames at any second. Then suddenly the carnival ride stopped, and the car came to a shuddering halt on its broad wheel base.

Frank glanced at his brother and Chet. "You guys okay?" he asked anxiously.

Joe moved his head back and forth gingerly, grimacing a little from the pain of a stiff neck. "I'll be all right."

Chet tried to force a smile and gave a thumbs-up sign. "I can't believe I almost got killed by a comic-book character," he muttered.

"Me either," Joe agreed. Seeing that they were all unhurt, he turned on the ignition to see if by some miracle the car still worked. The engine kicked on with a high-pitched screech that gradually died away, leaving an almost normal engine hum.

Frank was astounded. "Pretty good, considering that battering. Well, if this heap can make it that far, take us back to the spot where the Dreadnought pitched us over the cliff," he told Joe.

Peering through the fractured windshield, Joe drove the battered sedan along the bottom of the hill until he came to a spot where the incline leveled off. He shifted into low and made it back onto the road. In a few minutes they were back to the place where they'd blocked the alley.

Joe and Frank began examining the ground around them, while Chet stood nervously scanning the area.

"You don't think those crooks are still around, do you, Frank?" Chet asked.

Frank looked up from the dirt. "Afraid they'll come back?"

Chet nodded sheepishly. "A little. I don't mind helping you guys catch regular crooks, but fighting people with superhuman strength gives me the creeps."

Joe stood behind Frank, a scornful expression on his face. "Nobody's got superstrength, Chet! The Human Dreadnought is just a guy in a costume."

"But you saw him. He picked up our car and rolled it down the hill!" Chet sputtered.

"Joe's right," Frank stated flatly. "Nobody's strong enough to pick up a car with three people in it."

Frank waved Chet over to where he was kneeling and pointed to a pair of deep parallel furrows in the dirt.

"What do you think these are?" Frank asked.

"Tracks of some kind, maybe from something heavy," Chet guessed.

"Like what, Chet?" Frank prompted.

Chet shrugged. "How should I know? You're the detective, not me."

"Maybe those marks were made by whatever the Dreadnought was carrying when he got out of the van," Frank suggested.

"Which was probably a hydraulic jack. That's what he used to tip our car over," Joe added, "not superstrength."

Chet nodded dubiously. "I guess that makes sense. But why go to the trouble of faking superstrength? I don't get it."

Frank was quiet for a moment. "That's just one of the things we'll have to figure out."

Frank picked himself off the ground. "I've seen enough," he said as he dusted off his hands. "Let's swing by Kaner's home. Maybe we can find out something about what happened to Kaner before the kidnappers' trail gets too cold."

The trio got back into the battered sedan and Joe drove back to Lake Baca Drive, with the car clanking and squealing every inch of the way. When they arrived, Joe noted that the police cars parked before the Kaner home had been joined by several plain black sedans.

"They look like FBI cars," Joe guessed.

"How can you tell?" Chet asked.

"They're unmarked sedans. Standard FBI issue," said Joe.

"We might as well go back to the hotel now, Joe," Frank added. "I doubt we'll get to talk to Mrs. Kaner tonight."

"Yeah, the cops and FBI will keep her tied up for hours," Joe agreed.

The battered car protested loudly anytime Joe drove over thirty miles an hour, but he managed to coax it back to the rental agency without stopping. They decided not to tell the truth about what had happened to the car—who'd believe their story about the Dreadnought, anyway. The story they did tell convinced the manager to rent them another car after they filled out an accident report with the police.

Frank felt tired and discouraged as Joe pulled into the parking garage. They went upstairs, stopping only to pick up some soda and a few pretzels and chips at the snack bar in the lobby. Up in the Hardys' room, Joe sat on his bed while Chet flopped on Frank's bed. Frank took the straight-backed chair that stood in front of the small desk.

Pulling out a notebook and pen from his shoulder bag, Frank asked, "Chet, if this gang keeps impersonating Terrific Comics supervillains, what are some other characters we might run up against?"

Joe rolled his eyes in disbelief. "Frank, will you give this comic-book stuff a rest? I didn't think you actually believed we were up against real supervillains."

"I don't," Frank answered. "But it never hurts to have an idea of a criminal's possible methods."

Chet chewed a potato chip thoughtfully before answering. "Well, the Human Dreadnought is Terrific Comics' main villain, and Flame Fiend pops up a lot. They've got a character called Peregrine, too. He's a flying villain from the Green Cyclone comic. He's got a lot of advanced weaponry and a spaceplane," Chet explained.

Frank nodded, scribbling notes, then motioned for Chet to continue. Chet had finished the small bag of potato chips and was opening a bag of pretzels as he replied.

"There's Electro-man, who can throw lightning bolts and destroy electronic hardware. There's also Whip Scorpion, a really nasty villain from the Z-Crew comic. He wears flexible body armor and carries a bullwhip. He throws knives and ninja stars and can walk on walls and ceilings."

"Brother," muttered Joe, shaking his head. "I hope we don't have to tackle a big gang of costumed warriors. The two so far have been bad enough."

Frank paused, flipping through the pages of the notebook that he'd already filled. "Chet, do you know of any connection between Johns and Terrific Comics?"

Chet popped a pretzel into his mouth. "Hmmm—I think Johns used to work at T.C."

Frank made another note in his book. "What else do you know about that relationship?"

"Not much," Chet admitted, "but Tom could tell you. He's an expert on every phase of Johns's career. He knows a lot about Terrific Comics, too."

"Let's go talk to him," Joe suggested.

Chet checked his watch. "We've probably missed him. Knowing Tom, he's probably at a party. I doubt we could find him now."

Frank flipped his notebook closed. "There's not much more we can do tonight. What do you say we pack it in and go grab a pizza?"

"Dinner?" Chet beamed. "I thought you'd never ask."

Joe looked at Chet in amazement. "How can you even think about food after all the chips and pretzels you just put away?"

Chet just smiled. "That was only an hors

d'oeuvre, Joe. Now I'm ready for the main course."

The Hardys woke up early Friday morning. After quickly showering and dressing, they took the elevator to the lobby to meet Chet.

Chet arrived fifteen minutes late, bleary-eyed.

"You look like a man who didn't get much sleep last night, Chet," Frank observed.

"Good guess," Chet answered with a yawn. "Try three hours. I ran into some people, and we wound up talking and watching old monster movies in the film room till five. These cons are legendary for their parties. The con runs movies twenty-four hours a day. There's even a comic-con channel on the hotel's cable TV."

"Well, I trust you're awake enough to help us find Tom this morning after a visit to the convention center," Frank told him.

Chet yawned wide. "Sure," he said sleepily. "But I've got to have some breakfast first."

The trio devoured huge plates of pancakes and sausages at the hotel coffee shop, washing everything down with glasses of orange juice.

When they got to the lobby of the convention center, Frank saw that the fire damage had been repaired.

"That was quick work with the fire extinguisher," Chet commented. "The fire would've caused a lot more damage if it hadn't been for you."

Frank shrugged, his mind on the case. "Chet, since the two supervillains we've encountered are from Terrific Comics, how about a visit to the T.C. table?"

Chet led them into the main hall, where the comic-book publishers had set up booths and tables lined with comics and graphic novels. Behind their tables most of the publishers had colorful displays featuring either their stable of characters or the covers of various comics titles. The hall had just opened for the day, and there were only a few fans inside wandering around and leafing through comics.

Chet led the Hardys to the Terrific Comics booth. As they rounded the end of the aisle, both Hardys started in surprise at the sight of the Human Dreadnought, Flame Fiend, and several other characters they didn't recognize. All the characters were looming over a dark shape that was hunched over the table.

"What the—" Frank did a double take, but after a second he realized that the supervillains were simply life-size dummies in costume. Still, the resemblance to the men from the day before was unsettling. The man who'd been hunched over the table straightened up suddenly, and Frank saw that he'd been arranging rows of comics.

The dark-suited man turned in profile, and

Joe drew in a sharp breath. "Frank, that's the same guy who drove past Kaner's house right after the kidnapping!" he said quietly. He leaned over to Chet and whispered, "Chet, do you know who he is?"

"Sure, that's Harry Saul, president of Terrific Comics."

"Great," said Joe. Maybe they could get some information to help them discover who the villains were. Joe sauntered over to Saul and asked politely, "Can we speak with you a moment, Mr. Saul?"

Saul looked Joe over, then answered in a jovial tone, "Sure, kid."

As Frank and Chet joined Joe, Saul's dark eyes flicked over their faces before returning to Joe's.

"How well do you know Barry Johns?" Joe asked.

Saul's face hardened. "Why do you want to know?" he asked suspiciously.

"Did you know he's been kidnapped?" Joe asked.

Saul was obviously annoyed. "Of course I know! I was here at the convention. Don't waste my time asking dumb questions, kid!" he snapped.

"Don't you think it's a little strange that Johns's kidnappers were dressed up like your characters, Mr. Saul?" Frank asked.

"I don't know anything about it!" Saul

snarled. "If some crooks want to dress up like my characters, I have no control over that or them!"

"Didn't Johns once work for you?" Joe inquired.

Saul's shiny dark brown eyes flicked from Joe to Chet to Frank before he answered. "Yeah, so what? The little weasel used to work for me. It doesn't mean anything. Lots of people have worked for me besides Barry Johns."

"Most of your employees, past or present, don't get kidnapped, though. Isn't that right, Mr. Saul?" Frank asked.

Saul's face darkened with barely contained rage. "Look, Johns used to work for me, but that was years ago. I don't like the guy. He got kidnapped and that's too bad, but you won't find me shedding any tears over him. Now, if you three know what's good for you, you'll stay out of my hair! I have ways of dealing with people who annoy me!"

Chapter 5

HARRY SAUL SAT behind his table and crossed his arms.

"Wait a minute, Mr. Saul," Joe began, taking a step closer.

Frank laid a hand on his brother's arm. "Forget it, Joe," he said quietly. "I think he's told us everything he's going to."

"Now what?" Joe grumbled as he allowed Frank to lead him away from the Terrific Comics booth.

"We find Tom and see what he can tell us about Johns and Saul," Frank answered. Turning to Chet, he added, "Lead the way, Chet."

Chet took the Hardys into the dealers' room, where comics art was being bought and sold. The three boys wandered among rows of tables piled high with boxes of comics. They finally found Tom poring over stacks of Golden Age art.

"Hi, Tom," Chet greeted him cheerfully.

"Hey, Chet," Tom called. "What's up?"

Chet laid a big hand on Tom's shoulder and leaned in to say, "Frank and Joe need some inside info on the comics business."

"What do you want to know, guys?" Tom asked.

"About Barry Johns's relationship to Harry Saul and Terrific Comics," Joe told him.

Tom adjusted his glasses and glanced at Frank and Joe. "Johns began by writing fan letters and visiting the T.C. offices in the early seventies. Then, a couple of years later, he worked up some samples and began going around to the comics companies for work. He didn't have any luck until Harry Saul took him on as an office boy."

"An office boy?" Frank repeated. "When did Johns start getting his reputation as a writer and artist?"

"About ten years ago, while he was still at Terrific Comics," Tom replied. "But even the first year Johns worked there, he pestered Saul to let him pencil some comics."

"What do you mean, pencil some comics?" Frank asked, interrupting.

"Uh, well, since comic-book art's always been done fast, the work was usually broken up among a few artists. The penciler lays down the pencil art, then a letterer puts on the balloons and captions, and the inker draws in ink with a pen or brush or marker over the pencil."

"That's all fascinating, I'm sure," Joe said impatiently, "but what about Johns and Terrific Comics?"

"Anyway," Tom continued, "Johns wanted the work so bad he started out doing anything, lettering corrections, erasing pencil lines on inked pages, you name it. He worked hard, and Saul was finally impressed enough to give him a break."

"Uh-huh. Then what happened?" Joe asked.

"Johns penciled some short backup stories. He got good real fast and began getting a lot of fan mail. Pretty soon he was Terrific Comics' star attraction, penciling two of their most popular titles."

"Saul sure didn't have much good to say about his former boy wonder when we questioned him," Frank commented.

"That's because of the Metaman lawsuit."

"Metaman?" Joe asked, puzzled.

"The superhero. What happened was that after Johns worked for Saul for about four years, they had a falling-out and Johns quit. Then a couple of months later, Johns announced he was forming his own company, Zenith. Another guy, Dewey Strong, who'd worked for Saul for over twenty years, also quit, and went to work for Johns.

"Saul slapped Johns with a plagiarism lawsuit right after the first issue of *Metaman* came out," Tom went on. "He claimed that the character Metaman was a creation he'd been developing secretly, and that Johns or Strong stole it."

"Well, I can see why Johns wasn't popular with Saul," Joe remarked.

"Ah, but the story gets juicier," Tom proclaimed. "When the lawsuit finally came to trial, Strong testified that Metaman was Johns's creation. Saul lost the case, and now Metaman is Zenith's most popular character. Metaman comics made Johns a millionaire. There was supposed to be a Metaman movie, too. It would have made Johns ten times as rich if he'd finished making it."

Frank had been scribbling notes as Tom talked. Tom was being very helpful, Frank thought. Maybe his weird behavior after the fire had been a fluke.

"Saul's got a reputation for being very hot-tempered. He shoots his mouth off a lot, but he never actually threatened Johns as far as I know," Tom replied. "I do know that Johns and Saul haven't spoken since the lawsuit."

"All this makes Saul our number-one suspect," Joe stated.

"There's another thing, guys," Tom put in. "Saul's not the only person Barry Johns ever got in trouble with. He's got a reputation for not paying free-lancers and printers and a lot of other people, too, like letterers and colorists."

"Hmm," said Frank. "So Johns had enemies, but so far most of the circumstantial evidence points to Saul. Except for one thing.

Why would Saul use people dressed like his own characters to commit crimes? Wouldn't he be too shrewd to do something that obvious?"

"Saul does seem to have a bad temper, though, and bad-tempered people sometimes make mistakes. Why don't we see what else we can dig up on him, Frank?" Joe asked.

Frank thought for a moment. "Let's go and see Mrs. Kaner first," he said. "We need to know how her husband fits into all this. Maybe she can tell us more about Johns, too."

He turned to Chet. "Why don't you and Tom hang out and then catch some lunch. Joe and I will meet you back here in a couple of hours."

Chet shot him a quick thumbs-up sign, then turned back to Tom. "You going to the costume contest tonight?"

Tom laughed. "I never miss it."

The Kaner house looked much more peaceful than it had the previous day. The front lawn still bore the deep tire ruts, but Joe noticed that the battered front door had been replaced. He gestured up the street toward an unmarked car parked at the curb with two bored-looking men sitting in it.

"Except for the two plainclothes boys, it seems pretty deserted. Now might be a good time to go over there," Joe said.

"Yeah, but we'd better try the back door, so the cops don't see us. They might not understand that we're on their side."

Joe waited as Frank quickly stuffed his microcassette recorder into his shoulder bag, along with a new notebook, camera, and evidence envelopes. Then, keeping one eye on the unmarked police car, he and Frank casually strolled to the other side of the street and walked past the Kaner house until they found a wide alley that ran behind the rear of the houses. Joe knocked on the rear screen door. There was a long wait; then he saw a curtain beside the door part, revealing a pair of frightened pale blue eyes. The door popped open a few inches.

"What are you doing in my backyard?" the woman snapped.

"Are you Mrs. Sydney Kaner?" Joe asked politely.

"Who wants to know?" she shot back.

"My name's Joe Hardy, Mrs. Kaner, and this is my brother, Frank. We're investigating your husband's kidnapping."

"We'd like to talk to you for a few minutes, Mrs. Kaner," Frank added.

Mrs. Kaner peered at them suspiciously. "You're not the police. Who are you?"

"No, ma'am," Joe assured her. "We're not with the police, but we are detectives. We want to help get your husband back."

"You boys are a little young to be detectives," she said pointedly.

"Please, Mrs. Kaner," Frank said. "We saw

Barry Johns kidnapped yesterday, and if your husband was kidnapped by the same gang, he might be in for a rough time. Anything you could tell us would help us find his kidnappers."

"Well," she said reluctantly, "I don't know what I can tell you that I didn't already tell the police and those FBI men." And with that, Mrs. Kaner closed the door.

Joe was afraid that was it, that Mrs. Kaner wouldn't talk to them, but a moment later he heard the chain being unhooked, and the door swung open.

"Come on in, boys. I'm Amelia Kaner." The petite silver-haired woman was about sixty. "Sorry if I seemed rude, but with the reporters, the police, and the FBI, I haven't had much of a chance to recover my wits."

Amelia Kaner led them into the living room. The first thing the boys noticed was that there had obviously been a terrific struggle in that room. There was a hole in the wall, a smashed mirror was on its side, leaning against a wall, and an untidy heap of papers and books was laid haphazardly on an end table.

"Looks like there was quite a fight here, Mrs. Kaner. What happened?" Joe asked.

"Well," she began, "I was in the kitchen making dinner, and Syd was in the living room going over some papers. All of a sudden I heard a car drive right up to the front of the house, and the door split right down the middle. It made quite a crash, I tell you. Syd jumped up and shouted something like, 'Hey, what do they think they're doing?' Then a big man dressed up like a tank walked right into our house!"

Amelia Kaner stopped suddenly and buried her face in her hands.

"Take it easy, Mrs. Kaner," Frank said, putting a hand on her shoulder. "You don't have to tell us anything that upsets you."

"It's all right, son," she replied, meeting his gaze with sad eyes. "It's just that talking about it brings it all back so vividly."

She cleared her throat and sighed, then said, "Why don't I bring out some iced tea?"

"That'd be great," Frank said. "Let me help."

Mrs. Kaner led the way into the kitchen, and Joe heard Frank drawing her into conversation. As their voices retreated into the rear of the house, he started to check out the living room for any clue the police might have missed.

Going through the untidy stack of books and papers, Joe pulled a sheet of paper out and scanned it. It was a legal document, and on the top of the page were two names in bold type: Sydney Kaner and Jack Parente. They were the plaintiffs in a legal action against a third name that was prominently displayed on the sheet—Barry Johns.

Joe did a double take. Tom had said Johns

had a bad reputation with free-lancers, but here were two of his own staff suing him!

Joe started to read the document, but he knew Frank and Mrs. Kaner would be returning soon, so he slipped it back. Quickly flipping through the stack, he saw more legal documents and a few newspaper clippings about Johns.

Mrs. Kaner reentered the room, followed by Frank, who was carrying a tray with tall glasses and a pitcher of iced tea.

"Anyway, Mrs. Kaner," Frank was saying, "how did your husband like working at Zenith?"

"Syd's been very unhappy with Barry for the last year or two," she said delicately.

"Do you have any idea why?" Joe asked.

"Syd didn't share his work with me." Mrs. Kaner paused for a moment. "But I do know he felt he was being cheated out of royalties. That's about all. Sorry."

"Do you think he had any idea he was in danger?" Joe asked her.

Amelia Kaner shook her head. "Nothing he shared with me."

"What was his relationship with Harry Saul?" Frank inquired.

"Syd used to do some work for Harry from time to time. They got on all right, until Syd went to work for Barry. After that, Harry stopped talking to Syd." Amelia Kaner fell silent and took a long drink from her glass of tea. She lowered her eyes. Joe sensed they weren't going to learn any more from her. Catching Frank's eye, he cocked a thumb at the door. Frank nodded, then gulped down the rest of his glass of tea and stood up.

"Thanks for talking with us, Mrs. Kaner," Frank said, extending a hand to her.

"Yeah, and thanks for the tea," Joe added, coming to his feet.

"You're welcome, boys," Amelia Kaner told them as she showed them out.

As Joe and Frank went out the Kaners' front door and got into their car, they noticed the two sleepy-looking cops come alive. Just as Joe'd suspected, they weren't too tired to take notice of the Hardys. Joe watched one of the cops take down their license number, while the other one talked on the radio.

"Well, we know now that Kaner felt Johns was cheating him. Did you learn anything else while I was in the kitchen?" Frank asked.

"I saw some legal papers about a lawsuit with Kaner and someone named Parente, against Barry Johns," Joe told him. "The lawsuit could be over royalties, but I didn't have time to read it."

"Hmmm. I wonder if the kidnappers know there's bad blood between Johns and Kaner? Looks like the case has just gotten a lot more complicated," Frank said.

"Where do you think we should go next, Frank?" Joe asked.

Frank was chewing his lower lip. "The hotel, I guess," he answered distractedly. "But take your time, I want to hash the case out on the way."

"Suits me," Joe answered. He threw the car into gear and guided the sedan down Lake Murray Boulevard.

"Judging from that paper you saw, Johns seems to have a lot more enemies than we thought," Frank pointed out.

"Where do you suppose that stuff about Kaner's stolen royalties fits in?" Joe asked.

"I wouldn't even guess without more information," Frank replied. "I mean, judging from what we just found out, I'd say Kaner and Parente are suspects. But Kaner's a victim, too. It doesn't make sense. And another thing—I still don't understand why the crooks torched Johns's art collection." Frank shook his head.

"Maybe it was for revenge," Joe speculated. "It's one way Saul could get back at Johns and really hurt him."

"Possibly"—Frank shrugged—"but why not steal it and sell it?"

"Maybe the crooks had only enough time to set a fire," Joe suggested.

After an hour of driving and talking, Frank and Joe were no closer to solving the two kidnappings, so they drove back to the convention. Joe wasn't surprised to find Chet in the dealers' room with Tom. Both boys were hunched over a pile of plastic-wrapped Golden Age artwork.

"How'd it go, fellas?" Chet asked eagerly when he saw the Hardys.

"Well," Joe began, "we know more, but there are still too many blank pieces in the puzzle."

"I'd like to talk to some other people from Johns's staff and see how they felt about their boss," Frank put in.

"Try artists' alley," Tom suggested. "Dewey Strong is Zenith Publishing's main penciler. He's got a table there. Come on. I'll show you.

Joe, Frank, and Chet followed Tom to a part of the dealers' room where the tables had been arranged in big rectangles. The artists sat behind the tables on the inside of the rectangles. In front of them stacks of original comics pages were for sale, and there were a few hand-painted signs with the artists' prices for doing sketches.

Tom stopped and gestured toward a cartoonist in his sixties who sat in the center of a table facing the three boys. He was a medium-size, ruddy-faced man with a shock of uncombed white hair. He wore ink-stained khaki pants and a T-shirt with the figure of Metaman.

A mixed crowd of younger and older fans stood around watching as Strong sketched on a pad.

"That's him," said Tom. He walked over to the man and said, "Hello, Dewey. How are you?"

Strong's face split into a crooked grin. "Hi, Tom. How's the boy, huh?"

"Good, Dewey. Hey, listen, these are the Hardy brothers," he told Strong, then stopped to clasp Chet's shoulder. "And this is my pal Chet Morton, a big fan of yours."

"It's nice to meet you guys," Strong said. "Sorry, but I've got a lot of fans here waiting to buy sketches. I can't chat right now."

"We'd like a little of your time, Mr. Strong," Joe insisted.

"It's about Barry Johns's kidnapping," Frank added. "We need any information you can give us about Johns's enemies."

Strong's expression soured. Turning away from the Hardys, he carefully tore the sketch from his pad and handed it to a pudgy youngster wearing a vest covered with superhero buttons.

"Barry didn't have many enemies," Strong said slowly as he began a new sketch. He was obviously picking his words carefully. "I liked the guy. He always treated me okay. Now, if you'll excuse me, I've got a lot of sketches to do."

With that, Strong bent his head and concentrated on sharpening his pencil.

There was nothing more they could do, Joe realized. Strong would only ignore them until they left. He turned to Tom. "Is there anybody else at the con from Johns's staff?"

"Sure," Tom answered immediately. "Jack Parente is Zenith's head writer. He usually mans the Zenith public-relations table at cons."

"That's the other name from the lawsuit," Joe whispered to his brother.

"Then I definitely think we should talk to Mr. Parente. Let's try the exhibition hall," Frank suggested.

As the Hardys rounded the corner of an artists' table, a massive form suddenly planted itself directly in their path.

The first thing Joe noticed was that the black man in front of him was big. Hard muscles rippled under his conservative brown suit, and his white shirt was stretched tight across his broad chest. His dark eyes glittered with menace as he held up a hand.

"Not so fast, boys," rumbled the man's deep voice.

Joe drew in a sharp breath and took a step back.

He's big enough to be the Dreadnought, Joe suddenly thought.

Chapter 6

"WHAT'S GOING ON HERE?" Joe asked, trying to ignore how huge the man was.

"Pipe down, kid. I'm asking the questions," the suited man told him. The expression on his broad face was hard. He loomed over the Hardys as he asked, "You kids are Frank and Joe Hardy, right?"

Frank estimated that the guy stood a good half-foot taller than either he or Joe. Frank knew he'd be tough to take on in a fight.

"Mind identifying yourself before we answer that?" Frank asked.

With a bored expression, the massive black man flipped open a worn black leather wallet and flashed a San Diego P.D. detective's shield. "I'm Detective Sergeant Drew Hanlon. I'm working on the Johns kidnapping, and I have reason to believe you boys might have some information about the case."

Frank let out a sigh of relief. At least they wouldn't have to fight the guy. "I'm Frank Hardy, and this is my brother, Joe," he told the officer. "What do you want to know?"

"I'd really like to know why you two kids were badgering Mrs. Kaner."

"Badgering?" Joe practically shouted. "We weren't badgering anybody. She invited us in!"

"Keep your voice down when you're talking to me," Hanlon said sternly. "All I know is that when I called her today she sounded pretty upset. I asked her why, and she told me about your little visit."

Hanlon fixed the Hardys with a hard glare. "I don't know who you two kids think you are, but remember this. Kidnapping is a federal crime. I don't appreciate people who hassle witnesses in cases I'm working on. So just stay away from Mrs. Kaner."

"Sorry, Sergeant," Frank said in what he hoped was a humble tone. "We just thought we could help."

Hanlon snorted. "Maybe, just maybe, the San Diego P.D. can get along without your help. I know I can."

"We're not exactly inexperienced at investigating crimes," Frank told Hanlon. "Sometimes we work on cases with our father, Fenton Hardy. Perhaps you've heard of him."

Hanlon nodded. "Works on the East Coast. Yeah, I've heard of him. Good man. Fine detective," he said. "But that doesn't change anything. I still don't want you nosing around my case."

"But—" Joe objected, a rush of anger creeping up from under his collar and over his face.

Hanlon leaned over so that his face was only a few inches away from Joe's.

"Take my advice and keep away from this case. Me and the San Diego P.D. take a dim view of amateur detectives."

"Amateur!" Joe sputtered. "Why, you—"

Frank quickly stepped in front of Joe to prevent him from saying something that might get both of them into trouble.

"Don't worry, Detective," Frank assured Hanlon. "I'll see that we keep our noses clean."

"You'd better," Hanlon warned before turning on his heel and stalking off.

Joe glared at Hanlon's retreating back. "I don't like that guy," he announced to Frank. "He really rubs me the wrong way."

Tom and Chet, who had remained silent during the exchange with the detective, were relieved when Hanlon was out of sight.

Frank looked at his brother with a hard smile. "Let's find Parente. The clock's ticking on this case."

Finding the Zenith Publishing booth was easy. There was a huge life-size mural depicting Zenith's stable of characters, and above it, foot-high letters announced "Barry Johns's Zenith Publishing Co." It left no doubt as to where they were. The banner stretched behind three tables that were draped with red cloth. At one end of the table was a life-size cardboard standup of a smiling Barry Johns. Johns had a pretty big ego, Frank thought to himself. I wonder if he has the talent to match.

The Zenith booth was deserted. It didn't look as if anyone had been working all day.

"Parente's not here," he observed.

"Maybe he's in his hotel room," Tom suggested. "He's probably got a room at the Vasco. He always stays there during conventions.

Joe frowned. "I don't like the looks of this."

Tom looked uncomfortably from Joe to Frank. "Uh, there's something I should have told you before. About Johns's collection," he began.

Frank looked at Tom, wondering why he suddenly seemed to be so ill at ease. "What is it?"

"Uh, well, the fact is, the kidnappers didn't burn up everything in the collection."

"What do you mean?" Joe asked. "I saw what was left of it—nothing but ashes."

"Uh, not quite," Tom replied. He turned away, bent down, and began to dig through a black vinyl portfolio case bulging with artwork. A moment later he handed Joe a piece of illustration board; it had one charred side, but the top right-side corner was more or less intact.

"That's part of the original cover art for *Wonder Comics* Number Twenty-Three," Tom told him. "I saved it from the fire."

"That was a crazy thing to do!" Joe told him angrily. "It's evidence."

Tom gave a helpless shrug. "You've got to understand how it is with us original-art collectors. I saw my all-time favorite comic cover burning, and I just snapped. I tried to save what I could."

Only a small area of the art had survived, Joe noticed, but it clearly showed a part of a giant robot climbing over a crumbling skyscraper. He remembered it from the show.

Joe handed the cover to Frank, who examined it quickly. That explained why Tom had acted so shiftily right after the fire, Frank thought. He said, "You should have turned this over to the police."

Tom lowered his eyes. "I know. But after I took it, I was afraid I'd get into trouble, so I hung on to it. I didn't think anybody had noticed me take it."

"Look, if you're afraid of getting into trouble with the police, give it to us and we'll see that they get it."

Looking relieved, Tom gestured for Frank

to keep the charred cover. "Maybe it'll turn out to be an important clue," he said with a thin smile.

Joe was studying the cover as Frank held it. "It might be a good idea to get a list of all the artwork that was displayed. Maybe there's some connection between Johns's collection and his kidnapping." He turned to Tom and asked, "Tom, do you know everything that was in Johns's collection?"

Tom shook his head. "Not everything. But there's an art dealer who would, though. Morrie Rockwitz. Johns sold him some of his best pieces. He's one of the few people who knows Johns's collection better than me."

"Sounds like a good person to start with," Joe said with a grin. He turned back to his brother. "Frank, do you have your tape recorder handy?"

"Of course." Frank pulled it from his shoulder bag and handed it to Joe.

"I have a hunch I might need this today," Joe told him, slipping the recorder into the pocket of his brightly colored Hawaiian shirt.

"I think we should split up now," Frank told his brother. "I'll take Chet and see what we can learn about Parente. Why don't you two nose around the dealers' room and see what you can turn up?"

"Good idea." Joe nodded. "We can cover more ground that way."

The boys agreed to rendezvous back in the dealers' room in an hour. Then Frank and Chet went into the lobby to find a pay phone.

Frank punched in the number for the front desk of the Vasco and was quickly put through to Jack Parente.

"Hello," answered a gravelly voice with a faint trace of a Bronx accent. Frank thought the man sounded tense, on edge.

"Mr. Parente, my name's Frank Hardy. I'm a friend of Tom Gatlin's. He told me you were at the Vasco."

"Tom Gatlin." Parente's voice sounded slightly friendlier. "How is he? I haven't run into him yet at the con."

"He's fine, Mr. Parente," Frank replied. "The reason I called is that I'm investigating the Johns kidnapping. I'd like to talk to you."

There was a long, uncomfortable pause at the other end of the line. "That might not be such a healthy topic," Parente said finally.

"Look, I don't know if you're aware of this, but the kidnappers have a deadline, and it's running out. I don't think the police really have a clue where Johns is. If we don't find him first, he may wind up dead," Frank said forcefully.

"All right," Parente told him. "Come on up to my room. It's Room Three-oh-two. But make it snappy. I've got another appointment."

"I'll be there in a few minutes," Frank replied.

Suddenly Frank heard a tremendous battering sound at the other end of the line. There were sounds of voices shouting and sounds of a scuffle.

"Mr. Parente, are you okay?" Frank shouted into the phone. There was no reply, only another loud crash.

"Hello! Hello!" Frank shouted.

Then the line went dead.

"What is it, Frank?" Chet asked anxiously.

"I'm not sure, but whatever it is, it's bad. Come on!" Frank dashed across the lobby toward the plaza. He ran across Broadway toward the Vasco, dodging among conventioneers, tourists, and sailors from San Diego's big naval base. Chet followed as fast as he could but he was far behind Frank. By the time Chet puffed into the lobby, Frank had had time to get an elevator and was holding the door open.

Chet stumbled heavily through the elevator doors and slumped against the rear wall of the car, red faced and panting. Frank hit the button for Parente's floor, then turned to Chet.

"I hope we're not too late," he said, a grim set to his face.

When the elevator doors slid open at the third floor, they took off down the hall toward Parente's room.

The door hung open crookedly, and through the open space Frank could see two figures struggling inside. One of them wore bright red tights with a black hood, belt, and boots.

"It's Flame Fiend!" Frank shouted to Chet. "He's after Parente!"

Frank charged through the doorway. Parente was holding a chair in front of him for protection, but Flame Fiend had him backed into a corner. Flame Fiend turned and met Frank's eyes for a moment; then he eyed Chet. The two teenagers spread out and came at Flame Fiend from different directions. The masked kidnapper turned away from Parente to face Frank, who approached him in a combat crouch, his hands held in front of him, ready to parry any blows. Smiling, the criminal pointed his left hand at Frank with a flourish. Frank could see that Flame Fiend had something in his palm.

A second later fire shot from Flame Fiend's sleeve. Frank ducked, and the column of flame splattered on the wall behind him. Seconds later, the smoke alarm whined on.

Flame Fiend moved his hand to the left and set fire to the wall where the doorway was. Flames quickly covered the entire wall. The room's sprinklers came on, but the spray of water had little effect on the rapidly spreading flames.

The flame compound must be mixed with gasoline to burn like that, Frank thought. Quickly he turned back toward Parente, who was leaning against the wall with a dazed expression. Before Frank could do anything, Flame Fiend strode over to Parente and cut him across the jaw with a terrific right cross. Parente collapsed in a heap in the corner.

The red-costumed figure gestured again, this time hurling a shaft of flame that nearly struck Frank.

Then Flame Fiend turned back to the unconscious Parente and lifted him onto his shoulder. Laughing crazily, the criminal turned and strode through the wall of fire with Parente slung over his shoulder.

By now, choking clouds of smoke had begun to fill the room, and Frank began coughing as he breathed it in. Across the room he saw that Chet, too, was coughing and choking.

Suddenly Frank realized with horror that the deadly wall of fire that covered the exit was advancing on them. Flames leapt from the burning walls, driving Frank and Chet farther against the far wall. Heat scorched Frank's face, and he could feel himself growing dizzy from the choking fumes.

We're sunk. We can't get through the door, Frank thought. There's no other way out of this room!

Chapter 7

FRANK DOUBLED OVER in a sudden coughing fit. When he straightened up, he noticed a patch of blue next to him. It was just visible through the smoke.

In a flash he realized that the window looked out over the hotel pool. That's it! he thought. Grabbing the heavy desk chair Parente had been holding, he shouted, "Chet, follow me!" Frank swung the chair at the window with all his strength, smashing it outward in a bright shower of glass shards.

"We're going to jump for it, Chet!" Frank shouted over the roar of the fire.

"Out the window?" Chet shouted back, not believing his ears.

"It's our only chance!" Frank shouted.

The curtains framing the picture window had caught fire now and were flaring toward the boys. Chet scrambled up on the windowsill, Frank right behind him.

"Aim for the deep end," Frank told Chet.

Then Frank pushed off from the sill as hard as he could. He heard Chet's yell right beside him.

"*WHOOOAAA!*"

Frank cut the water cleanly, sinking almost to the bottom of the pool's deep end, then kicking straight back to the surface. Almost numb and sputtering for breath, he looked wildly around for Chet, and was relieved when he saw his friend bob to the surface.

Chet choked on the water as he made his way to the pool's edge.

"Boy, that was a cannonball to end all cannonballs!" he gasped.

"At least we're alive," Frank told him.

Suddenly Frank was aware of being the focus of attention of a growing crowd. "Chet, everyone's staring at us," Frank muttered out of the corner of his mouth.

The perimeter of the pool was rapidly being filled by comic conventioneers, some of them already dressed in the costumes they would wear in that night's costume contest.

"I've got an idea, Frank," Chet whispered. "Just follow my lead."

Chet stroked over to the nearest ladder and

hauled himself out of the water. As Frank followed him, Chet bowed deeply to the crowd, and the conventioneers immediately applauded and cheered. The cheering increased as Chet turned to another portion of the crowd.

Frank smiled disbelievingly. "Chet, why are they cheering for us?" he whispered as he joined his friend.

"Because we made it into the pool from a third-floor window," Chet explained with a smile. "They think it was a stunt."

Just then Frank caught a fleeting glimpse of a face that set off warning bells. He twisted his head around to get a better look, and sure enough, it was the familiar hawk-nosed profile of Harry Saul.

Saul was staring up at the third floor, where flames billowed out of the window of Parente's room. The crowd suddenly noticed the flames all at once. A girl screamed, and in the distance, Frank heard the high-pitched wail of a fire truck as it approached the hotel.

Frank's eyes flicked back to where Saul had been standing, but he was gone.

Frank wanted to get out of his wet clothes, but he knew he had to report Parente's kidnapping and the fire to the authorities right away, so he and Chet stopped at a pay phone in a back stairwell and called Sergeant Hanlon's office. Then Frank and Chet returned to their hotel rooms to change clothes.

Frank called the convention center and had Joe paged, and within fifteen minutes the three boys had reassembled in the Hardys' room.

"I heard about your daredevil leap into the pool. Are you okay?" Joe said as soon as he'd walked through the door. His blue eyes were shining with excitement.

"We're fine, Joe," Frank assured him. "But the kidnappers got Parente."

"What? Those crooks seem to be everywhere!" Joe said in frustration. After a pause he added, "Well, at least I picked up more info about Johns."

"Is it a lead on the kidnappers?" Frank asked eagerly.

"Nope," Joe replied, "but it is interesting."

Joe took a can of cola from the mini refrigerator in their room and took a long drink.

"I was talking to Morrie Rockwitz, this art dealer who used to deal with Johns."

"What'd you learn?"

"He didn't tell me much," Joe said. "He admitted he'd bought and sold Golden Age artwork with Johns over the years, but he didn't seem too eager to tell me anything else. He did accidentally let me see something real interesting, though," Joe added.

"When I walked up to his table, it was deserted, and Rockwitz was standing behind it studying a piece of artwork. As soon as he noticed me, he slipped it into a big art portfolio, which he left unzipped, fortunately."

"Why fortunately?" Frank asked.

Joe tilted his head back to drain the rest of his soda before answering. "Because when I glanced down into his portfolio I saw a Golden Age cover that supposedly got burned up with the rest of Johns's collection!"

Frank's eyes widened. "Are you sure of that, Joe?"

"Positive," Joe replied firmly. "It was the same cover Tom managed to save part of—the corner from the one with the giant robots. And that means—"

"One of them must be a fake," Frank cut in. "Did you ask Rockwitz about the cover?"

"No, but as soon as he saw me notice it, he got real nervous. He started sweating a lot, and then ended the conversation in a hurry."

"Oh, yeah?" Frank asked. "I think I'd like to talk with this Rockwitz guy."

"You can't," Joe told him. "Right after I got finished talking to him, he left the dealers' room. He made some kind of excuse about a meeting."

"I think we should track him down," Frank said. "There's something funny going on with Johns's art collection. Somehow this collection is tied in with the kidnapping.

"Leave him to me, Frank," Joe said confidently. "Once we find Rockwitz, I can play him like a violin."

Frank grimaced. "Cut the drama, Joe."

"This case is getting more complicated by the minute. First a kidnapping, then two, then three, and now maybe art forgeries to boot. It beats me how we're going to solve this one before our time runs out."

Frank nodded. Obviously, one of the covers was a forgery, but which one—the one that got burned or the one Rockwitz had? Could it be that Johns had sold Rockwitz some fakes? If so, maybe Rockwitz was involved in the kidnappings. Or maybe Rockwitz was working with Harry Saul. But what about Kaner and Parente? Where did they fit in? Frank shook his head. One thing was sure—they needed more information.

"We're up against a gang of pros, Joe," Frank commented. "But like Dad always says, 'To catch crooks, you've just got to outthink them.' " Turning to Chet, he asked, "Is there anyone else from Johns's staff that we can talk to?"

"Dewey Strong," Chet replied. "He's been on Johns's staff longer than anybody."

"You mean that artist we saw this morning?" Frank asked. He frowned, remembering how Strong had given them the cold shoulder. "He wasn't exactly eager to talk to us."

"We've got to give it another try," Joe insisted. "We don't have any choice. Come on. Let's head back to the dealers' room."

When the boys returned to the table where

Strong had been earlier, he wasn't there. When Frank and Joe asked about him, they were told Strong had left.

Joe frowned, then turned to Chet. "Do you know where Strong lives?" he asked.

"No, but I bet Tom does."

Chet and the Hardys found Tom in another corner of the dealers' room, sorting through a stack of Golden Age artwork.

"What's up, fellas?" Tom inquired as he saw the boys approaching.

"We need Dewey Strong's address," Joe told him.

"Sure." Tom bent over, zipped up his portfolio case, and picked it up. "I'll take you there," he told them.

"Great," said Joe.

Twenty minutes later Joe rounded the corner of the street that Dewey Strong lived on. Tom pointed out a five-story brick apartment building at the end of the street. Behind it was a fifteen-story steel-and-glass monolith that dwarfed Strong's building.

Joe came to a halt in front of the apartment building, and the four boys hopped out and headed for the entrance. The front door of the building was unlocked and the lobby was empty, so Frank, Joe, Chet, and Tom simply got on the elevator and rode to Strong's fifth-floor apartment.

As soon as the elevator doors opened, Joe saw that one of the apartment doors had been kicked in, just like the doors in the other kidnappings.

He sprinted down the hall and into the apartment, which was a shambles. All the furniture was overturned, and the floor was littered with books, broken glass, and the scattered pieces of a chess set. The TV was hissing on a dead channel, and a framed comic-book cover hung at a crazy angle on the wall, its glass smashed in a jigsaw puzzle of cracks. He felt a sick sensation of dread in the pit of his stomach as he scanned the room.

Joe's attention was drawn to something in the center of the wall: a note pinned to the wall with a steel ninja star.

"That's just like the ninja stars Whip Scorpion uses," Joe heard Chet say behind him.

Joe reached for the star to pull it from the wall, but a hand clamped around his arm, stopping him.

"Don't touch it, Joe. You'll smudge the prints," Frank insisted.

Pulling out a handkerchief, Joe wrapped it around the star and pulled it from the wall. He carefully set the star down, then opened the envelope, using his handkerchief. The note inside was in word-processor printing on plain white paper, like the first ransom note, Joe recalled.

We want $100,000 for Strong. If all ransoms are not paid by midnight tomorrow, he will die with Kaner and Johns.

Whip Scorpion

As he finished reading, Joe heard a crashing thump overhead. He shouted, "Someone's on the roof!"

Joe ran out into the hall and headed for the red exit sign at the end of the hall. He ran up the wide, twisting stairwell to the roof, hearing Frank a few steps behind him.

Joe threw open the door to the roof with a loud bang, startling two people climbing up the corner of the adjoining building. They were about eight feet off the roof of Strong's building. Joe recognized one of them as Dewey Strong. His abductor looked like a creature from another planet—or from the pages of a comic book, Joe thought wryly. He wore a black costume that featured flexible bands of body armor around his legs, arms, and torso. His head was covered by a grotesque black insect-head mask topped with antennae. He held Strong with one arm locked around his chest, and the other twisting Strong's left arm behind his back. But in the gathering dusk, it was hard for Joe to see exactly what was going on.

Joe sprang into action and scrambled up a big air-conditioning duct. Strong's legs were still within reach, so he grabbed both of his ankles and tugged. Backing up the wall, Whip Scorpion began to pull on Strong's upper body, but Joe hung on determinedly.

Suddenly Whip Scorpion kicked away from the wall and released Strong's upper body. Joe knew he couldn't hang on to the wiry old cartoonist, so he let go of Strong's legs, too. Joe winced as he heard Strong hit the roof with a loud thud.

Then, before Joe had a chance to react, Whip Scorpion leapt and swept Joe from his perch. He held him in a hammerlock.

Joe heard Whip Scorpion whisper, "Haul me up," and then his words were followed by a burst of static. Joe felt himself being jerked up into the air, and then Whip Scorpion pushed off from the side of the tall building.

Caught in Whip Scorpion's iron grip, Joe swung out over the edge of Strong's building in a wide arc. Far below he could see the street and sidewalk. Suddenly Whip Scorpion pushed off from the building again and let go of Joe.

Joe yelled and watched in horrified fascination as the pavement far below rushed up at him.

Chapter 8

JOE FELL PAST FRANK, then was lost to sight.

"Joe!" Frank shouted.

Frank heard a loud crash below. He and Chet and Tom rushed to the edge of the roof and looked down. Joe was several feet below them, dangling by one hand from a bent metal bar supporting some solar panels that were bolted to the front of the building.

"Joe!" Frank yelled again. He tried to reach his brother's hand, but Joe dangled several feet out of reach.

"Hurry, Frank!" Joe called.

Just then the bar Joe had grabbed on to bent with a screech, dropping Joe another foot closer to the ground.

"This thing won't hold!" Joe shouted. "Get me up, quick!"

Frank turned to Chet. "Chet, you've got to hold my ankles while I grab Joe!" Frank felt Chet's strong grip on his ankles, and he wormed his way over to the edge of the roof to hang down headfirst. Joe's outstretched right hand was only inches below his grasp.

"Drop me down a little, Chet," Frank called. He felt his friend ease him a few inches lower, just enough so that Frank managed to grab Joe's wrist in both his hands. Joe let go of the support and grabbed Frank's right arm.

"Pull us up!" Frank ordered through gritted teeth.

Chet gave a mighty heave. Sweat beads popping from his forehead, he rocked back and slowly pulled Frank toward him.

A moment later Chet saw one of Joe's hands suddenly appear on the edge of the roof, then the other hand, then Joe's face, grimacing as he hauled himself up.

When his brother was safely on the roof, Frank let go of him. "You all right, Joe?" he asked with concern.

Joe moved his legs and arms around gingerly. "My right arm almost got pulled out of the socket," he said, "but I'm still breathing."

Frank saw that there were some scratches

on Joe's face and arms, but there didn't seem to be any serious injury.

"Man!" Joe said. "Another second and I would have been testing my flying skills!"

The joke suddenly reminded Frank of the costumed kidnapper, and he looked over at the next building. In the dim purple-and-orange glow of sunset, he could make out no movement, but he thought he saw a slender glint of metal along the side of the building.

"They got away again!" Frank exclaimed in frustration.

"Yeah, but at least they didn't get Strong," Joe reminded him. "Let's see how he is."

Joe, Frank, and Chet joined Tom, who was bent over Strong. Strong lay on his side unmoving, his eyes closed, his face a rigid mask of pain.

"How is he?" Frank asked Tom, kneeling down by him.

"His leg might be broken. I don't know what else," Tom said.

"Chet, call an ambulance. You and Tom wait here with Strong. Joe and I will join you at the hospital later," Frank said.

"They'll probably take him to Saint Mary's. It's three blocks from here," Tom said as the Hardys turned to go.

Frank and Joe talked their way into the neighboring apartment building by explaining to a bewildered security guard about the kidnapping attempt. On the roof they found a large winch chained to an upright drainpipe.

"Here's the cable Whip Scorpion descended on," Joe observed, pulling up a length of strong steel cable.

Frank held up an aluminum mountaineer's D-ring. "He must have rappelled down the side of the building, then gotten hauled up with the winch for a quick getaway."

Joe joined him beside the winch. "Any clue as to where this equipment came from?" he asked.

"Nope." Frank pointed to the side of the winch, where an identifying metal plate had been pried off. "They took off the nameplate and filed away the serial number. This stuff's clean as a whistle."

Disappointed, Frank and Joe left the apartment building, and after a quick supper drove to Saint Mary's Hospital, where they joined Tom and Chet in Strong's room.

Strong's leg was broken and in an elevated cast; he was dressed in a white hospital gown. The old man looked sleepy from the sedation, but Frank thought he saw Strong's expression brighten when they came in.

"How're you doing, Mr. Strong?" Frank asked.

"I'm alive, thanks to you Hardys," Strong

replied. "At least that's what Tom and Chet told me."

"Do you have any idea who these kidnappers are?" Frank asked him.

Strong's face hardened. "No, but I got a pretty good idea who hired them—Harry Saul! There's a lot of bad blood between Saul and Johns. It'd be just like old Harry to use his characters to get back at the enemy."

"Sounds pretty fantastic," Joe observed.

"Harry's about the meanest son of a gun I ever met," Strong said quietly. He paused. "Besides, I know where there's proof."

"Proof?" Frank asked urgently.

"A letter," Strong told them groggily. His voice was fading as the sedative was making him sleepier. "A couple of days before the kidnapping, I saw Barry reading a letter. He got—real scared. Told me—told me afterward it was a threat from—Saul."

Strong's voice became an inaudible whisper. Frank thought he'd fallen asleep, until Strong opened his eyes a crack. "Take my keys— Go to—the Zenith offices— Letter's in Barry's desk—"

Joe found the keys in Strong's pants, and the Hardys, Chet, and Tom left.

Out in the hall Joe tossed Strong's keys up in the air and caught them with a snap.

"You must be raring to go to find that letter, Joe," Frank said with a grin.

To Frank's surprise, Joe shook his head, and an intensely thoughtful expression came over his face. "That can wait," Joe said. "I have a hunch that now might be a good time to double back to the con and find Rockwitz."

Frank opened his mouth to argue, then changed him mind. Usually, when Joe had one of his hunches, it was worth acting on.

The dealers' room was abuzz with talk of the kidnappings when Joe, Frank, Chet, and Tom returned. Chet and Tom went off by themselves, while Joe led Frank toward the far end of the room, where he'd spoken to Rockwitz earlier that day.

The room was packed and Joe and Frank made slow progress. They were constantly forced to sidetrack around thick groups of conventioneers who were examining and buying artwork. They still hadn't reached Rockwitz's table when they ran into Tom, who was upset.

"Frank, Joe, I've got to talk to you right away," Tom said.

"What's wrong?" Joe asked.

"I just got offered a piece of artwork that I know has to be either stolen or a fake," Tom said miserably.

"What?" Frank asked.

Tom bit his lip and squinted uncomfortably behind his wire-framed glasses. "I went over to Rockwitz's table, but it was a mess. A lot of his artwork was packed in boxes. I asked what was up, and he tells me he's leaving the con early.

"But then he comes over and says that since I've been such a good customer, he's going to offer me a special deal," Tom went on. "He pulls out the *Wonder Comics* cover with the giant robots from Johns's art collection."

Joe shot a knowing look at his brother. That was the same cover he'd seen earlier.

"Go on, Tom," Frank said, nodding.

"So I say to him, 'What this? This piece of art got burned on Thursday.' Rockwitz just laughed. He offered it to me for a thousand bucks. That's about a tenth of what it's worth. Said he had to unload it quick. Rockwitz wouldn't be selling it at such a low price if there wasn't something shady going on."

Joe's mind clicked into action.

"We better get over there fast," Joe said to Frank.

When they got to Rockwitz's table, it was almost bare. Rockwitz was moving with frantic haste as he piled boxes in a low cart. When he caught sight of Joe, his face grew pale.

"Can't talk now, guys," Rockwitz said with a nervous look. "Got to go. There's been a—uh, death in my family. Uh, so if you'll excuse me . . ."

Joe stepped right in front of Rockwitz and shook his head. "No, you don't. You're not going anywhere until you answer a few questions."

Rockwitz stared at Joe and dismissed him with a shrug. "I don't have to talk to you. You're not the cops."

"No," said Frank, leaning across the table, "but they might be interested in an art dealer who's involved in fraud."

"Tom told us you offered him one of the pieces of art that supposedly got burned yesterday. What's going on with Johns's art collection?" Joe asked in a hard voice.

"Nothing. There's nothing illegal going on," Rockwitz said quickly. "Johns sold me some stuff from his collection, but it was all perfectly legit. What he did on his own after he sold me the art is none of my concern. I'm just an honest businessman."

"Maybe not so honest," Frank put in. "If Johns ever tries to get the insurance money for phony work, then you're an accessory to insurance fraud."

Rockwitz's mouth fell open. He started sweating heavily, clearly rattled.

"Just tell the truth, Morrie," Joe prodded. "If you know anything about Johns, it could help us solve his kidnapping."

Rockwitz sat down abruptly as if he'd been

deflated. "Okay," he said softly. "What do you want to know?"

"First things first," Joe told him. "What's the story with the burned artwork?"

"All that stuff was fake!"

"How do you know?" Frank asked.

"It had to be! I bought Johns's whole collection," Rockwitz told them.

Frank and Joe exchanged glances.

"When?" Joe asked.

"He started selling it off four or five years ago. He sold more of it every year until about two weeks ago, when he sold me the last big batch of it. I paid him a lot of money for it, but Johns acted like the money almost didn't matter. He was acting weird that day, distracted."

"Did you know the fakes were going to be burned?" Frank asked.

"No!" Rockwitz replied indignantly. "I'm just an art dealer, not a crook! I didn't even know there *were* any fakes until I arrived at the convention. I was pretty steamed when I saw the display, but Barry was kidnapped before I could talk to him about it. And after—well, I didn't want to end up in the same boat he's in, so I kept my mouth shut."

It seemed to Frank that Rockwitz was telling the truth, although he couldn't be sure until he'd asked Sergeant Hanlon to have his lab check the charred cover to determine its age. Frank rubbed his chin as he and Joe and Tom walked away from Rockwitz.

"What is it?" Joe asked. "Did you figure something out?"

"Not yet," Frank replied.

Noticing that Tom was hanging on their every word, Joe said, "Tom, could you find Chet? Tell him we'll meet him at the hotel later."

"Okay," Tom said, and a second later he disappeared into the crowd.

"Good," Frank said. "We need to go over what we already know."

Joe ran a hand through his sandy blond hair and blew out a long breath. "Whew! Where do we start?"

Frank pulled out his notebook and ran a finger down a page of notes. "Okay. One. We know that Johns, Parente, and Kaner have all been kidnapped by unknown persons disguised as *Terrific Comics* supervillains. Two. We know Harry Saul hates Johns, maybe enough to kidnap him, and that he probably wrote Johns a threatening letter."

"Besides which he was seen near Kaner's house and Parente's hotel at the times of their kidnappings," Joe added.

"Three. We also know that Johns secretly sold his art collection to Rockwitz before it got burned, and that means there could be some kind of scam to get Johns's insurance money," Frank said. "Maybe it's the insurance money that the kidnappers are after."

Frank scanned his list again. "Four. The kidnappers' deadline runs out at midnight tomorrow. That doesn't leave us much time."

"Let's go to Zenith Publishing now and find that letter Strong mentioned," Joe suggested. "If the letter is there, we might be able to pin the kidnappings on Saul and save Johns before the deadline runs out."

Frank stowed away his notebook. "Let's go."

The midtown San Diego area where Zenith Publishing was located wasn't far from the convention center. Since it was late, it was totally deserted. Frank checked out the area carefully as he drove up to the rear of the building. If there was trouble, they would be on their own. "I want to park this thing somewhere inconspicuous," he told Joe.

"Okay. I'll open the Zenith offices." Joe got out of the car. "Meet you inside."

Frank parked behind a Dumpster, then slipped inside the building, locking the door behind him.

He tried to call an elevator to the ground floor, then realized the elevators must be turned off for the weekend. Spotting an exit sign glowing in the corner, he headed for it. Swiftly but quietly, he went up the stairwell, pausing at every landing to listen for any noise.

The building seemed totally silent. Joe must already be upstairs, Frank decided. Letting out a long breath, he flexed away some of the tension that had built up in his back muscles and continued up the stairs.

Suddenly the stairwell shook violently, throwing Frank against the wall. A huge explosion rocked the floor just above him.

Chapter 9

FRANK FELT HIS LEGS buckle under him, and he hit the stairs hard. The explosion left a ringing in his ears, but he stood up and knew he wasn't hurt. As Frank shook his head to clear the ringing, he realized . . .

Joe!

Frank hurried up three or four stairs to get to his brother, but the stairs above these were blocked with rubble from the explosion. A heavy feeling of dread grew inside him as he surveyed the debris blocking his way.

The blast had knocked Joe to the floor of the Zenith reception area. Though slightly stunned, Joe knew to roll under the receptionist's desk and wait till the explosion died away.

When everything was still, he crawled out from under the desk to see what kind of damage the explosion had caused. There was shattered glass everywhere, and at the opposite end of the floor an office was on fire. Long tongues of flame shot through the shattered doorway. It was probably Johns's office, Joe figured, but there was no way he was going to take the time to make sure. The Zenith bullpen, with its rows of desks and drafting tables, wasn't burning yet, but it would be soon. It was a good place, Joe decided, to get out of quickly.

Joe picked his way carefully over the broken glass, stepping around the overturned chairs and other debris that littered the reception area. He blew out a sigh of relief when he made it into the darkened hall. As he walked toward the stairwell at the other end of the hall he could see in the dimness that the explosion had blown out one wall of the office, completely blocking the stairwell from below with a heap of brick and chunks of plaster. Smoke was billowing into the hall from the hole in the office. Somewhere on the floor, Joe heard a fire alarm screech on.

"Joe! Joe! Are you okay?" The frantic shout came up through the piles of rubble, and Joe had to strain to hear Frank. Cupping his hands around his mouth, he shouted back, "I'm okay, Frank! Not a scratch!"

"Can you get down?" Frank called.

"Not here! The explosion knocked out the stairs below me!"

There was a tense moment of silence; then Frank called up, "Take the stairs to the roof! I'll take the fire escape and meet you there!"

Joe scanned the stairs leading up, then answered, "All right. The stairs going up look good! See you in a few minutes!"

Once on the roof, Joe took a deep breath to clear his lungs of smoke. Then he looked around the roof until he spotted the fire-escape ladder on the opposite side of the roof. He walked toward it, but paused halfway there when he heard something behind him.

Before he could turn around, Joe felt a sudden stinging sensation around his ankles and his feet were pulled out from under him. He fell hard, and the wind was forced from his lungs in a single breath.

Joe immediately rolled over onto his back to see who his attacker was. In the darkness it was hard to make out details, but Joe did recognize the insect helmet and shiny black costume banded with body armor—Whip Scorpion!

He saw that Whip Scorpion held a long bullwhip in his right hand, and that the end of the whip was wrapped around Joe's ankles. Kicking free, Joe rolled behind an air-conditioning duct.

Crack! The whip struck only a few inches

from Joe's head. As he dodged reflexively to the left, Joe's hand passed over a length of rusty pipe and he grabbed it, grateful for the weapon.

Whip Scorpion snapped the whip at Joe's head again, but Joe blocked the blow with his piece of pipe. He tried to pull the whip away, but it flicked all round him too fast.

Joe was sweating in the cool night air as the Scorpion's whip drove him toward the edge of the building. Where was Frank? he wondered. The whip cracked again and Joe dodged, taking a step backward, closer to the edge.

Joe saw Whip Scorpion draw back his arm for another strike. He tensed, ready to dodge or parry it, but the crook had frozen in place, his arm locked in position over his head.

Joe looked past Whip Scorpion and saw Frank with one hand tightly gripping the tip of the bullwhip. Whip Scorpion tried to yank the whip from Frank's grasp, but Frank jerked back on it, throwing Whip Scorpion off-balance.

Knowing he'd never get a better opportunity, Joe lunged at the crook with his pipe and struck a glancing blow on the side of the insectlike helmet, causing Whip Scorpion to stagger backward.

Frank yanked on the whip again, but to Joe's surprise, Whip Scorpion easily jerked it from his grasp, then turned two backflips and landed lightly on his feet in front of Frank.

Before Frank had a chance to react, Whip Scorpion landed a right cross to his jaw that sent him reeling. Then Whip Scorpion scuttled down the fire-escape ladder.

Joe threw down his pipe and charged after Whip Scorpion. He descended the ladder two steps at a time, determined not to let the crook escape. Joe saw Whip Scorpion stop on the landing below him and pull something shiny from his belt.

"Duck!" Joe heard Frank call from above.

Joe ducked, and narrowly missed being hit by a five-pointed ninja star, which clanged off a fire-escape rung.

Just then, a nondescript white sedan appeared at the entrance to the alley and screeched to a halt near the bottom of the fire escape. Joe saw Whip Scorpion start at the sight of the car, but he didn't slow down, even when a huge, dark figure popped out of the driver's side of the car and brandished something in the air.

"Police! Hold it!" the man shouted.

Whip Scorpion ignored the command and vaulted down to the bottom landing, nimbly catching himself at the last instant. He hung there for a second, then somersaulted into a pile of cardboard boxes behind the Dumpster.

The dark figure fired a warning shot in the air as Whip Scorpion sprinted toward the end of the alley.

Joe watched from the fire escape as a silver van roared up to the mouth of the alley. Dreadnought's angular helmet was clearly framed by the open driver's window. A split second later the door on the side of the van slid open, and Whip Scorpion dived in. The Hardys heard the van's powerful engine rev, then the tires screech as it raced off.

In the next instant the dark figure spotted Frank and Joe on the fire escape. He swiveled and pointed his revolver at the boys, standing in a marksman's crouch.

"Freeze or I'll blow you away!"

Chapter 10

FRANK AND JOE raised their hands.

"Don't shoot," Frank called out. "We're unarmed."

"Come down where I can see for myself," the dark gunman commanded in a strangely familiar voice. "And keep your hands where I can see them."

"Play it cool, Joe. This guy seems edgy," Frank said in a low voice as he caught up with Joe. Frank and Joe reached the bottom of the fire escape and dropped lightly to the ground. The gunman stepped out of the shadows. It was Sergeant Hanlon.

"What are you two doing here?" Hanlon demanded angrily, lowering his gun.

There was an awkward silence, which was

filled by the loud whine of an approaching siren.

"Well, speak up," Hanlon told them.

Joe broke the silence. "We were checking out a lead in the Johns case, Sergeant. Dewey Strong gave us his keys to the Zenith offices so we could see a threatening letter Johns got a few days ago."

"And I suppose you don't know anything about the bomb your buddy set off," Hanlon said sarcastically.

"Our buddy!" Frank said incredulously. "Detective, we were chasing that guy!"

Hanlon gestured for them to come forward. "Yeah. Sure. Tell me about it at the station house."

"I've already told you, Sergeant. We went to Zenith to look at a letter Johns got from Harry Saul," Frank said, feeling his exasperation growing. They had already been in the station over an hour, but Hanlon was still giving them a hard time. They'd told him what Strong had said about the letter from Saul, and had filled him in on all they knew about Johns, Kaner, and Parente.

"Look," Frank said, trying hard to keep a lid on his temper. "We're trying to cooperate. What else do you want to know?"

"Anything you guys have learned about

Johns that might have a bearing on this case,'' Hanlon responded.

"Did you know Saul was in the vicinity of the Kaner kidnapping?'' Joe asked suddenly.

"Or that he was also nearby when Parente got kidnapped from the hotel?'' Frank added, remembering that he'd seen Saul in the crowd after his leap into the pool.

Hanlon nodded and made some notes on his pad.

"Here's another angle you may want to look into,'' Frank told Hanlon. "Where's my bag? There's a piece of evidence that I want to give you.''

Hanlon got up and left the room, returning a moment later with Frank's bag. Frank opened it and pulled out the scorched page fragment Tom had given him.

"Okay, I'll bite. What is it?'' Hanlon asked.

"It's a piece of art from Johns's collection that got burned during his kidnapping,'' Frank replied. "We think that piece of artwork you're holding is a forgery.

"Can you have it sent to the police labs to test the age of the paper?'' Frank asked. "If it's less than fifty years old, it's a forgery.''

"Forgery?'' Hanlon shook his head quizzically. "Wait a minute, I thought we were dealing with kidnapping here.''

"It's more complicated than that, Sergeant. Johns has been selling off his art collection to one art dealer," Frank explained. "We think it's possible that Johns replaced the art with forgeries so it would look like he still owned them."

Hanlon made several notes, then looked up at the Hardys with a flinty expression. "Maybe I was a little hasty calling you boys amateurs. You've turned up some real interesting information. But smart or not, you're still civilians, and if you stick your noses into police business, I'll arrest you for obstructing justice. Got me?"

"We understand, Sergeant. We'll stay out of your way," Frank said, hoping that Hanlon would believe him.

To Frank's relief, Hanlon sat back in his chair and dismissed them with a wave. "Okay, then get out of here. I don't want to see you guys around this case again. I mean it!"

"Hey, guys, are you okay?" Chet asked.

The Hardys had found him browsing the convention art show, on the floor above the dealers' room. Frank was surprised the exhibits were still open, but then remembered what Chet had said about the weird hours of comic-book cons.

"We ran into Whip Scorpion on the roof of Johns's building right after the bombing," Joe said.

"Whip Scorpion! What happened?" Chet asked.

"He got away, and we ended up getting hauled down to the station house by Sergeant Hanlon," said Frank.

"Have you learned anything new, Chet?" Joe asked.

"The kidnappings are the talk of the con, but nobody really knows much. What I'm hearing is mostly rumors about Harry Saul."

"Well, it seems like all roads lead to Saul," Frank cracked. "I have a feeling we won't get much more done tonight. How about hitting the sack so we can make an early start tomorrow?"

"I'd like to eat something first," Joe replied. "I'm so hungry, those stale doughnuts on Hanlon's desk were starting to look good. You want to join us, Chet?"

Chet shook his head. "Nope. I'm meeting Tom in a little while so we can hit the costume contest. Hey," he added, "if you're knocking off working on your case, why don't you guys come with us? The San Diego Con costume contest is one of the best in the country. Some of the costumes are amazing!"

Frank shook his head. "Sorry, Chet, I'm just too beat. Nearly getting blown up does that to me."

"What about you?" Chet asked, turning to

Joe. "There are bound to be plenty of pretty girls in the contest."

Joe looked as if he might consider it, but then he, too, shook his head. "Chet, you know I hate to be a wet blanket, but if I don't catch some Z's tonight, I'll be worthless. Besides, I've already seen enough costumes for one day."

"Today's the day the kidnappers' deadline runs out, Frank," Joe said the next morning. "Where to first?"

"To see the only person connected with the kidnapping we haven't talked to yet, Barry Johns's wife. I heard her name was Phoebe," Frank replied.

The Hardys got their car from the hotel garage, stopping only to buy a bag of sweet rolls and two large glasses of juice.

With Frank navigating, Joe pulled their blue sedan up in front of the Johnses' home half an hour after leaving the hotel.

Frank and Joe got out and rang the bell beside the front door of the large ranch-style house.

"Who is it?" a woman's voice asked from a small speaker next to the doorbell.

"We're Frank and Joe Hardy, ma'am. We're investigating your husband's kidnapping," Frank answered.

There was a short pause; then the door swung

open and the Hardys found themselves staring at a tall, pretty, dark-haired woman. She quickly sized up the Hardys. "If you're reporters, you should leave now. I'm not talking to any more of you people," she said sharply.

"We're not reporters, we're detectives," Joe reassured her. "We just want to help find your husband."

"Please, Mrs. Johns, we need your cooperation if we're going to save your husband before the deadline runs out. There's not much time," Frank told her.

"You boys seem like a long shot to me, but at this point I'll try anything." Phoebe Johns's face remained stern, but she stood aside to let them in. Silently she led them through the ultramodern house to a large living room furnished with black leather-and-chrome chairs and an expensive-looking black leather sofa. The Hardys took the chairs, and Phoebe Johns perched on the edge of the long sofa, looking at them tensely.

"Did your husband ever say anything about being afraid of Harry Saul?" Frank inquired.

"Barry rarely mentioned Harry after they had their falling-out," Phoebe Johns said.

"Do you think Harry Saul is the kind of guy who'd kidnap your husband for revenge?" Joe asked bluntly.

Phoebe Johns's expression hardened.

"I'm sorry, Mrs. Johns, but we have to ask

these questions if we're going to find your husband in time," Frank said uncomfortably.

"I don't know what I'll do if you don't find him," she told the Hardys. "I can't possibly pay the ransom."

"What!" Frank and Joe said simultaneously.

"I'm broke," Phoebe Johns said tightly. "After I saw the ransom note, I called our bank. They told me all our accounts were empty except for a few hundred dollars in the household checking account."

"But everyone I've talked to assumed Barry Johns was rich," Frank said.

"I never paid much attention to our finances. Barry handled everything. And until now, I've never wanted for anything. Maybe that's where a lot of our money went. Barry was so status-conscious. He always had to look like a big success and have the best of everything."

Joe thought for a moment, then asked, "Did your husband gamble, Mrs. Johns?"

She shook her head. "No, Barry never went in for that sort of thing. Though he did take a couple of gambles recently."

"What do you mean?" Frank asked.

"Business gambles. He lost a large sum of money on the Metaman movie. I'm not sure how much, but it was a lot, because Barry insisted on producing the movie himself."

"Did your husband have any other unsuccessful projects recently?" Joe asked.

Phoebe Johns thought for a moment. "There was a toy deal the year before, to merchandise his characters as action figures. That was a big disappointment. He got very irritable and preoccupied after that deal fell through."

"But if Zenith Publishing was as successful as we've heard, your husband could have afforded a few setbacks," Frank pointed out.

"Zenith was successful, but Barry plowed a lot of the money back into the business. The last few years, he's been complaining about how his labor costs eat up most of his profits."

"Wait a minute," Joe cut in. "I thought Barry Johns was famous for writing and drawing his own comics. Why did he need to pay his staff so much?"

Phoebe Johns looked down at her lap. "Barry used to do two or three books a month, but lately, running the business has been taking up so much of his time that he had Kaner and Parente ghosting most of his work."

"What's ghosting, Mrs. Johns?" Joe asked.

Phoebe Johns sighed wearily, then explained, "A ghost is someone who does work for an artist or writer but lets the other person sign his name to it. Barry wouldn't talk about it with me, but I knew he couldn't work. He was burned out. For months he just couldn't come up with any new ideas. Jack Parente was writing all the titles Barry was supposed to be handling."

Frank listened intently. Everything Phoebe Johns was telling them only confirmed all they'd heard about trouble between Johns and his staff. But what was the connection between Johns's business troubles and Harry Saul? That was one thing that just didn't make sense, even though Saul obviously had the biggest motive for wanting Johns kidnapped.

Changing the subject, Frank asked, "Do you know where the kidnappers want the ransom delivered?"

"Not yet." Phoebe Johns shook her head. "The first ransom note said only that they'd contact me."

She abruptly stood up. "Since I don't know when the message is coming, I want to be ready for—whatever comes next. I'll have to ask you boys to excuse me."

Frank and Joe stood up and said goodbye. "Don't worry, Mrs. Johns. We'll find your husband in time, I promise," Joe said.

As they walked out to their car, Joe tossed Frank the car keys. "Why don't you drive back to the hotel, Frank?"

Frank caught the keys. As he and Joe got into the car he saw a metallic glint at the top of the hill. He thought he saw a flicker of movement, but it was so quick he couldn't be sure that he actually saw anything.

He was steering up the hill from the Johns

house when he looked ahead, and his mouth fell open.

The Human Dreadnought was standing at the top of the hill, and he was hefting a giant boulder with his bare hands. Frank couldn't believe what he was seeing. The Dreadnought braced himself with his left leg forward, then leaned back, holding the boulder high overhead.

"What the—" Frank began, but he stopped short when, with a mighty effort, the Dreadnought threw the boulder in their direction.

The huge boulder hit the street not far from the Dreadnought and rolled right toward their car, picking up speed as it bore down on them.

"It's going to plow right into us, Frank!" Joe shouted.

Chapter 11

FRANK CUT THE WHEEL sharply to the left, careening off the road and onto a green lawn just as the boulder rolled by. He slammed on the brakes, just missing a wrought-iron lamppost. He got the car under control and brought it to a halt back on the road.

The Hardys jumped from the car as the boulder continued down the hill, heading straight for the Johnses' house.

"Frank, it'll cream the house! Mrs. Johns—"

The huge stone bounced up over the edge of the sloping curb, then rolled right up against the front of the house.

Joe tensed, prepared to see a hole in the house. But although the boulder made a loud crash when it hit, it wasn't very destructive.

Joe looked quickly up the hill, but as he'd expected, the Dreadnought was gone. Then he and Frank raced back down the hill to the house.

There was no visible damage. The boulder had bounced and was sitting in the front yard a few feet from the house. Joe went over to examine it.

"Hey!" he called to Frank. "It's a fake! This boulder's made from some kind of plastic."

Frank came up to stand beside his brother, and when he rapped on the side of the boulder with his knuckles it made a hollow sound. "It's fiberglass, Joe, like the prop boulders in movies."

The front door of the house opened, and Phoebe Johns stuck her head out.

"What's going on?" she asked fearfully.

"You just had a visit from the kidnappers," Joe told her. "One of them rolled this into your house."

"Hey, what's this?" Frank asked, dropping to his knees beside the boulder. There was a ripping sound; then Frank turned to his brother, holding a heavyweight manila envelope with strips of silver tape stuck to either end.

"Looks like duct tape," Joe noted.

Frank shook his head. "It's gaffer's tape. Electricians in movies use this to attach stuff to light stands."

"Interesting," Joe said. "Another movie connection."

Phoebe Johns held out her hand. "Give me that envelope."

Joe and Frank both watched closely as she tore it open. Inside was a piece of white paper with a computer-printed message:

> Deliver the ransom in $20s, $50s, and $100s to the garbage can near the stern of the *Star of India* by midnight. Come alone. No police, or your husband and the others will be killed instantly.
>
> The Human Dreadnought

"The *Star of India*'s that old sailing ship moored down by the Embarcadero, isn't it?" Joe asked his brother.

Frank nodded. "Putting the ransom drop-off along the waterfront allows the kidnappers plenty of ways in and out of the area."

Phoebe Johns looked down at the ransom note blankly. "I can't pay this," she said in a flat voice. "What am I going to do?"

"I think the first thing you should do is go inside and sit down," Frank told her. "Then I think you should call Sergeant Hanlon and tell him about this note."

Phoebe Johns nodded. "I'll do that."

"We'd appreciate it if you could do one thing for us, Mrs. Johns," Joe told her. "Don't mention our visit to Hanlon. He doesn't really understand that we're only trying to help."

"Boys, if you can rescue Barry, I'll do whatever I can to help you. Right now, I don't have much confidence in the police or the FBI." With that, Phoebe Johns turned and went inside her house, locking the door behind her.

"If the cops or FBI are coming, we'd better make ourselves scarce, Frank," Joe said, starting to move back up the hill toward the car.

Frank held up his hand to stop him. "Hold on a minute, Joe. I want to take a closer look at this boulder."

Frank went to the boulder and rolled it completely over so he could see all of it.

"Aha!" he exclaimed.

Joe hurried back over, and Frank showed him a flat rectangular area on the boulder.

"What is it?" Joe asked.

"I'm not sure," Frank replied. He took out his pocketknife and began scraping the paint off the flat area, exposing a small impression that read, Luxor Special Effects Corp., S.D., Calif.

Frank showed the impression to Joe. "We'd better check out this Luxor Corporation," he said.

Joe spotted the Luxor Special Effects Corporation as soon as he turned their car onto the street where it was located. It was a huge warehouse with a snarling gargoyle, seemingly made of stone, projecting from the front of the building. Joe shook his head as he and Frank got out of the car and headed for the entrance. If this is California architecture, you can have it, he thought.

The first person they ran into was a dark, athletic-looking man wearing jeans and a cut-off sweatshirt.

"Can you tell us where to find the head honcho?" Joe asked.

The dark-haired man nodded. "That'd be Dave Wolfe, and you're looking at him. What can I do for you guys?"

"Just a little while ago we almost got run over by a giant boulder with your company's name on it," Frank told him.

Wolfe's bushy eyebrows shot up. "A boulder, huh?" he said. "Was it about eight feet across?"

"That's it," Joe replied. "How'd you know?"

"It was stolen from here about a month ago," Wolfe explained, "along with a bunch of other stuff. I'm still making an inventory for the insurance company."

Frank pulled out his notebook. This might be the break they'd been waiting for. "Do you have any idea who did it?" Frank asked.

"Yeah, but it was such a slick job I can't prove it. I think it was Lenny Goldson, my old pyrotechnics man. The burglary happened a few months after I fired him," Wolfe told him.

"Why was he fired?" Joe asked.

"His special effects always looked good, but he was careless. On the Metaman flick, an explosion went off prematurely and a couple of stuntmen had to go to the hospital with burns."

"Did you work with Barry Johns?" Frank jumped in.

"Sure," said Wolfe. "Johns produced it. But the picture was never finished. Johns ran out of money. I got paid, but a lot of other people didn't and are still suing Johns to get their money."

Frank's brow furrowed and he chewed his lower lip. "Mr. Wolfe, did Barry Johns and Lenny Goldson meet while making the picture?" he asked eventually.

"Yeah," Wolfe answered. "They were on the set at the same time for a couple of weeks. Why?"

"Just wondering," Frank said, quickly adding, "Can you tell us what else was stolen from here?"

"Yeah," Wolfe replied with a shrug. "If you're really interested. Come on." He turned and went into the warehouse, waving for the Hardys to follow him. Leading them to a cramped, tiny office at the rear of the warehouse, Wolfe showed Frank and Joe a clipboard with a sheaf of typewritten sheets on it.

"Here's a mostly complete list of what was stolen," Wolfe told them.

Joe scanned the top sheet and gave a low whistle. "That's a lot of equipment, Mr. Wolfe."

Frank leaned over Joe's shoulder. "Yeah, and look at what *kind* of equipment—power winches, a wind machine, a couple of compact hydraulic jacks, smoke grenades, lasers, and a mini-flamethrower!"

Joe ran his eyes down the list with growing excitement. Here was the break they'd been hoping for. The kidnappers had used most of the equipment on the list of stolen goods. Joe's mind clicked into action, fitting the pieces together. There were several hydraulic jacks on the list. No doubt the Dreadnought had used one of them to tip their car down the hill. The winches, cables, and mountain-climbing gear on the list had been used by the gang to make it seem like Whip Scorpion "crawled" up the wall of the big building.

Joe pointed to the mini-flamethrower noted on Wolfe's list. "That's got to be the one Flame Fiend used," he said excitedly.

"Mind telling me what you're talking about?" Wolfe asked.

Frank shook his head. "I can't really say right now, Mr. Wolfe. But trust us, it's not just idle curiosity."

"If Lenny Goldson is mixed up in something, then I'd steer clear of it. He isn't somebody to mess around with," Wolfe warned, his dark face serious. "Ever get a look at him? Goldson's six-feet-six and weighs about two-eighty, all muscle. He's a championship-level bodybuilder."

"He sounds big enough to be the Dreadnought," Joe told Frank. Turning back to Wolfe, he asked, "Do you know where we can find him?"

Wolfe looked skeptical. "It's your funeral, guys. Personally, I wouldn't come within a mile of Goldson. He's bad news."

Wolfe checked his address file and wrote down Goldson's address and phone number, handing the paper to Joe.

"Did Goldson have any close friends that you knew about?" Frank asked Wolfe.

"Lenny wasn't a very friendly guy," Wolfe answered, "but I guess he was pretty chummy with a couple of stuntmen who worked on the Metaman flick, Ted Basilio and Wally Trent. They're bad news, too. Ted used to work as a knife thrower in a circus, and he still likes to toss knives around. Wally's pretty weird, too. He used to do all the fire stunts Lenny rigged, right? But even off-camera, he was always playing with matches, you know? Doing little magic tricks and stuff."

"Thanks for the information, Mr. Wolfe," Frank said, jotting down the names in his notebook. "If we're going to track down Goldson, we'd better get going."

Wolfe nodded and led them toward the front of the warehouse.

As they made their way through the assortment of fake boulders, racks of monster costumes, catapults, and medieval war machines, Wolfe turned his head and said, "Oh, yeah, there's something I forgot to tell you guys about Goldson—"

Wolfe stopped in midsentence as a loud creaking sound cut the air. "Hey, what's—"

Joe turned toward the noise and saw that one of the war machines, a wheeled rack containing twenty arrows, was bcing trained on them.

In the next instant his blood ran cold as he heard the screech of the arrow catapult being cocked!

Chapter 12

JOE DIVED FOR WOLFE, tackling him out of range of the arrows, which whistled harmlessly overhead. Joe looked around for his brother.

"Frank!" he called out, sudden fear chilling him. "Frank!" he yelled again.

A tall shield leaning against a pile of suits of armor stirred and fell to the floor, revealing Frank.

"You okay?" Joe asked worriedly.

"I'm fine," Frank answered. "We better move and get whoever cocked that—"

The sound of clattering at the front of the warehouse drew the boys' attention. Frank and Joe took off instantly in the direction of the sound, with Wolfe lumbering behind them.

Flame Fiend was framed in the huge open doorway of the warehouse, freeing himself from a tangle of plastic pipe he'd stepped in. When he saw the Hardys and Wolfe approaching, he turned and fled up a ladder on the outside of the building.

"He'll escape over the roof!" Wolfe cried.

Joe reached the ladder first and scrambled up, with Frank close behind. Wolfe shouted, "I'll call the cops!"

Joe and Frank climbed as quickly as they could, keeping their attention on the scarlet form ahead of them. When Flame Fiend reached the roof, he sprinted along a narrow catwalk at the edge of the warehouse's sloping roof. Joe was still about fifty yards behind when Flame Fiend came to the edge of the building. Flame Fiend hesitated only a second before he hurled himself across a five-foot space to land on the flat roof of the neighboring warehouse.

Joe was right behind him. When he came to the edge of the Luxor warehouse, he paused just long enough to gauge the distance before jumping. Seconds after Joe's leap, Frank, too, landed safely on the other roof to follow Joe and Flame Fiend.

They ran the length of that building, then leapt off it to land heavily on a lower, flat-roofed building next to it. Frank realized with satisfaction that he and Joe were gaining on Flame Fiend.

Flame Fiend had now reached the door that led to some interior stairs. Luck was with the Hardys, and the door was locked from the inside. Cursing, the costumed man turned to flee, but the heel of his black boot stuck in a glob of sun-softened tar, and he fell flat.

Frank saw Joe pounce with lightning speed, grabbing Flame Fiend by the shoulder, but Flame Fiend lifted his left palm toward Joe and let loose a blindingly bright burst of light. Then Flame Fiend struck Joe across the temple, and Frank saw his brother slump over.

Before Flame Fiend could do anything more, Frank leapt on him from the side. But in the next instant Frank yelled in pain as his eyes were dazzled by a burst of searing white light. He swung blindly at Flame Fiend, who dodged easily and came back with a strong left to Frank's jaw. Frank felt consciousness slipping away. He managed to grab the sleeve of Flame Fiend's costume, and felt something tear as he blacked out.

When Frank opened his eyes, he saw Joe sitting near him rubbing his temple and shaking his head to clear it. Frank rubbed his aching jaw and searched the immediate area. Flame Fiend had vanished.

"I can't believe it!" Joe raged. "We almost had him!"

"Well, at least he didn't make one of us into

a human pincushion, or fry us," Frank commented. "That is funny—he could have fried us with his flamethrower, but he didn't. I wonder why?"

"Maybe he couldn't, Frank," Joe suggested. "Maybe the flamethrower and that dazzle gadget he used just now are too heavy to carry at the same time.

"Good guess, Joe," Frank said. "I just wonder what his 'dazzler' was."

After the Hardys made their way back to the Luxor warehouse, they described their battle with Flame Fiend to Wolfe.

"Yeah," Wolfe said with a nod. "That sounds like an effect I came up with for the Metaman movie. The gear for it was stolen, too."

"How does it work?" Frank asked.

"It's pretty simple," Wolfe told them. "Under your costume sleeve you wear a small laser that fires into an optical fiber that runs down to a flexible plastic mirror in the palm of your hand. You can fire the beam in any direction, depending on where you point the mirror."

"Does it weigh much?" Frank asked.

"The laser doesn't," said Wolfe. "But the power pack for it weighs about thirty pounds."

Frank extended his hand to Wolfe. "Thanks, Mr. Wolfe. Your help has been really valuable."

Wolfe started to shake Frank's hand, then snapped his fingers.

"Oh, yeah, I almost forgot! I was starting to tell you another place where you could find Goldson, when that crazy character fired the catapult. Goldson usually works out at Hercules and Company, a health club on the corner of Front and Hawthorn streets."

The Hardys decided to head back to the convention center to pick up Chet before checking out the health club. If Goldson was as dangerous as Wolfe said, they would need all the help they could get. Frank spotted Chet sitting alone behind Rockwitz's table in the dealers' room. A tall stack of artwork was piled in front of him. Rockwitz wasn't there.

"Hi, Chet. What are you doing behind Rockwitz's table?" Joe asked.

"Tom and I are keeping an eye on Rockwitz's stuff for him. Tom'll be right back. He just went to get some sodas."

"Where's Rockwitz?" Joe asked.

At that moment Tom came running up to the table. "You wouldn't believe who I just saw Rockwitz with," he said breathlessly. "Harry Saul."

"Where?" Frank asked.

"I saw them in the lobby, so I followed him into the little parking lot just outside the lobby," Tom explained.

Frank gave Joe a startled look. The theory that Saul and Rockwitz were in on the kidnappings together was suddenly sounding more probable.

"We'd better check this out," Joe said, moving toward an exit.

"Stay here, Chet," Frank called over his shoulder. "We'll be right back."

They ran past startled conventioneers into the lobby. Frank spotted the door Tom had mentioned, and motioning for Joe to be quiet, he cautiously opened it a crack, scanning for any sign of Saul and Rockwitz.

At the other end of the parking lot, near the street, Frank saw Saul and Morrie Rockwitz standing beside a green BMW. Saul seemed agitated. He was talking heatedly and shaking his fist in Rockwitz's face.

Rockwitz backed away from Saul and shook his head. He said something Frank couldn't hear and started to walk away, but Saul stepped toward Rockwitz and grabbed him by his T-shirt. Rockwitz pulled away easily and strode off. Saul started to go after him, but caught sight of Frank watching him. He glared ferociously at Frank, then turned and stalked back to his car.

"Let's see if we can persuade Saul to talk to us," Frank said to Joe.

But as Frank stepped through the doorway, Saul's green BMW took off.

"What about Rockwitz?" Joe asked. "Where did he go?"

Frank scanned the direction Rockwitz had taken, but he had disappeared, too.

"Gone," Frank said. "And we don't have time to look for him. It's almost four already. Let's get Chet and head over to Hercules and Company."

Frank checked his watch as he, Joe, and Chet ran toward the convention-center parking lot.

"The address Wolfe gave for Goldson's gym is only a few blocks from here, Joe. How fast can you get us there?" He was uncomfortably aware of how little time they had until the kidnappers' deadline ran out at midnight.

Joe grinned over his shoulder at his brother. "How's Mach Three?" he quipped.

Joe jumped behind the wheel and in a flash they were heading down Second Avenue toward the gym. As they weaved through traffic, Frank turned to Chet to ask, "What did you guys learn today, Chet?"

"Rockwitz wasn't kidding when he said Johns had sold him his entire collection. We went through the last batch of art Rockwitz says he got from Johns, and we found the originals for about half the pieces that supposedly got burned up on Thursday."

"But remember," Frank cautioned, "we still don't know which ones are fakes, the ones Rockwitz has or the ones that got burned."

"Here's the gym," Joe announced. He pointed out a three-story redbrick structure right on the corner of Front and Hawthorn streets.

"Keep your head up, Chet," Frank cautioned.

Joe pulled the car into a metered parking space. "Dave Wolfe warned us the guy we're going to see is a pretty rough customer."

The boys entered the building's lobby, and after consulting the building directory, Frank punched the button for the third floor.

"Chet, you stay in the lobby and keep an eye peeled for Goldson's accomplices," Frank instructed.

He and Joe rode the elevator to the third floor, and a pretty redhead wearing a Hercules & Co. T-shirt directed them to the weight room.

Frank said, pausing before going in, "Wait a minute, Joe. If Goldson really is the Dreadnought, as we suspect, he'll probably recognize us."

Joe clapped Frank on the back and said, "Don't sweat it, Frank. Goldson's big, but he can't take both of us."

The weight room was huge, with wood floors and overhead fluorescent lighting. It was empty except for a huge muscular blond man sitting at a Nautilus machine.

As Frank and Joe approached the man, Frank sized him up. He couldn't help wondering if they were making a big mistake approaching the guy so directly.

"Hi," Joe said, flashing a friendly smile.

The man returned the smile, but his eyes were cold and beady.

"Hello," he said in a deep voice.

"Aren't you Lenny Goldson, the special-effects wizard?" Frank asked, adopting an eager, fanlike tone.

"Yeah, that's right, fellas," he said in a cheerful gravelly voice. Then Goldson's hand shot out, hitting Joe in the chest and sending him tumbling backward over a weight-lifting bench.

Frank jumped on Goldson's broad back and locked his hands under Goldson's arms and behind his head in a hammerlock.

Goldson strained against the hold, and Frank felt his grip slipping. Goldson was able to reach around to grab Frank. The next thing Frank knew, he was being flipped over onto his back, and Goldson was towering over him, holding a thick stack of weights overhead.

Joe managed to scramble to his feet. He looked around wildly for a weapon. Grabbing a weight bench, he charged Goldson, holding it in front of him like a battering ram.

He rammed Goldson as hard as he could, letting out a kamikaze yell, and the big man keeled over, dropping the weights to the floor with a splintery crash. Despite the force of the blow, Goldson got back to his feet fast.

By now Frank had gotten to his feet, and he was circling around beside the larger man.

"Goldson!" Frank shouted.

As the big man started to turn his head, Frank's hand flicked out and clipped him on the side of the neck.

Goldson dropped like a stone and lay on the wooden floor, breathing heavily.

"Boy, Wolfe was right about Goldson. I don't think either one of us could have handled him alone," Joe said.

"You're probably right," Frank replied, wincing as he massaged his temple. He glanced down at Goldson's unconscious form. "I'd better call Hanlon right away. You keep an eye on Sleeping Ugly here."

Joe was watching Frank go through the doorway into the lobby, when he felt something close around his ankle and pull. He fell forward hard, barely catching himself on his hands. With a quick twist of his body, Joe managed to roll away from Goldson. He readied himself for the next attack—but it never came.

The massive weight lifter had whirled around and was charging through the swinging double doors that opened into the lobby.

Joe took off after Goldson, reaching the lobby in time to see Frank run for the stairs.

"I'm right behind you!" Joe called.

Frank ran down the two flights of stairs to the main lobby at top speed, but when he got there he found Chet sprawled on the floor, and Goldson's broad back disappearing through the front doors of the building.

"He blindsided me!" Chet complained as Joe appeared behind his brother. Frank helped Chet up, then threw open the front doors just in time to see Goldson leap into a red Mercedes convertible. The Hardys quickly piled into the front seat of their rental car, with Chet hopping in the back.

"Don't lose him, Joe," Frank said.

"Ha!" Joe responded. "No way! That car is like a big red Follow-Me sign."

Goldson sped south on Front Street, weaving in and out of slower traffic.

"He's driving like a maniac!" Frank shouted.

"He's going to shake us unless we go as fast as he is!" Joe replied.

The Hardys' sedan shot into the passing lane and roared forward, but they were still half a dozen car lengths behind Goldson's convertible. Joe poured on the speed to try to catch up.

The red Mercedes made a quick right at the next traffic light, and Joe managed to follow just as the light turned red, taking the corner with screeching tires. The gap between the Hardys' car and Goldson's Mercedes was narrowing.

"Yaa-hoo! We've got him!" Joe cheered. At that moment Goldson made a sharp left turn and disappeared down a wide alley next to an old factory.

"He's not losing me with that trick!" Joe said between gritted teeth as he spun the wheel hard to the left.

As soon as they turned the corner of the alley, Frank saw that they were in trouble. Not only had the red convertible vanished, but the alley was a dead end!

Joe slammed on the brakes, but Frank knew with dead certainty that they'd never stop in time.

Frank breathed in big gulps of air, trying to fight down the fear he felt as the brick wall at the end of the alley loomed larger by the second.

Chapter 13

"BRACE YOURSELVES!" Joe shouted. Frank and Chet sat back in their seats and threw their arms up in front of their faces. An instant later the car smashed into the brick wall—and easily tore right through it.

Joe kept his brake floored, and the car fishtailed to a stop inside a cavernous, dimly lit factory. It was only then that he realized the wall was a fiberglass-and-wood fake that had given way under the car's impact.

Joe finally remembered to breathe as he turned off the ignition. He checked to see if Frank and Chet were all right and watched as Chet fought to unbuckle his seat belt. Frank was opening his door. They both seemed to be dazed but unharmed.

"Well," Frank said as he cautiously slipped out of the car, "if they went to the trouble of concealing this entrance, there must be something back here."

Joe nodded, then pointed into the factory's dim interior. The aerodynamic shape of a new van was visible. It was being painted tan, but half of it was still silver. Behind the van, Joe made out the shape of a small hydraulic jack mounted on four small metal wheels. Goldson's red Mercedes was parked just beyond the van. The engine was turned off, and the driver's door was open.

"I think we hit the jackpot, guys," Frank whispered. "Stay sharp. Goldson should have heard that crash, and he may be ready and waiting for us. Fan out and let's search," he said. "But take it slow and easy. This could be a trap."

"Oh, I'll be careful, all right," Chet said. "This dump gives me the serious creeps."

Peering around cautiously, Joe crept over to the half-painted van. He peeked through the open side door, but there was nothing inside except a drop cloth, a couple of cans of spray paint, and a compressor and paint-spraying equipment.

At Goldson's Mercedes Joe glanced inside and saw on the front seat a garage-door opener. Of course! That explained how Goldson had gotten in. The "brick wall" rolled up into the ceiling and was operated from a standard opener.

"Joe, over here." Joe glanced up at the sound of his brother's voice and saw that Frank was standing beside a computer. A work station had been improvised, with the computer resting on a makeshift table of boards and sawhorses. Frank pointed to the back of the computer monitor and read "Property of Zenith Publishing. Do not remove from premises."

"The kidnappers must have stolen it from Zenith when they bombed the place," Joe said, keeping his voice low.

"I don't think so, Joe," Frank whispered. "There's something about this that strikes me as funny. Look," he said, tearing off a sheet of paper that stuck out of the printer. "Doesn't that type look like the ransom notes?"

Joe examined the letters on the page and nodded that Frank was right. He told Frank about the garage-door opener.

"Joe, Frank, over here," Chet called, interrupting them in a hoarse whisper. He was holding a length of cable like the cable the crooks had used to make Whip Scorpion "crawl" up the building wall. Joe looked up and saw that it was suspended from an overhead rafter and had a mountain climber's D-ring attached to the hook at the end. The cable ran to a winch that was identical to the one they'd found on the roof of the apartment building.

"This must have been where Whip Scorpion practiced his wall crawling," Frank speculated.

"I'd feel safer if we'd found Flame Fiend's flamethrower," Chet said with a nervous smile. "Then I'd know it wasn't pointed at us. Where is that Goldson? He had to hear us."

"Easy, Chet," Joe whispered reassuringly. "Maybe he thought we wouldn't follow him down the alley—he might not have heard us. But if we keep moving, it'll be hard for them to sneak up on us."

Frank pullcd a pcnlight from his shoulder bag and set off into the dark area of the huge factory. He quickly swung the beam of his flashlight along one wall of the factory, and it fell on some small equipment sheds. Then he switched it off.

He pointed to the sheds, indicating that they should check them out. Joe and Chet nodded.

The first shed was locked with a stout padlock. His ear pressed against the door, Frank could hear rustling and indistinct muffled tones.

"I think someone's in there, Joe," he whispered excitedly.

"Do you have any lock-picking tools in your magic shoulder bag?" Joe teased.

"No, but I saw a screwdriver over on that bench. We can take off the hinges."

Joe worked as quickly and quietly as he could, and within a minute he pulled the door open. Frank stood behind him, shining his penlight into the shed.

In the bright circle of light Joe saw a man with a white gag tied around his mouth. His wrists and ankles had been bound with gaffer's tape. The bound man lay on a beat-up cot in an empty storeroom.

Frank quickly tore away the gag.

"Thank God you've come," the man said in a feeble voice. "I was afraid they'd kill me."

Joe and Frank helped the man up into a sitting position. Then Joe slashed the tape around his ankles with his pocketknife, and Frank did the same to the tape around the man's wrists.

"Are you Syd Kaner?" Frank asked.

The man nodded. "Who're you guys?"

"I'm Joe Hardy, and this is my brother, Frank," Joe answered.

"I'm Chet Morton," Chet added. "I've always been a big fan of your work, Mr. Kaner."

Joe glared at Chet. "Save the hero worship, Chet," he said. "We're not out of the woods yet."

While Frank helped Kaner stand, he asked him, "Are any of the other kidnap victims here?"

"I don't know," Kaner replied. "I was blindfolded when I came in, and they've kept me locked up in this room."

Frank turned to Joe. "Let's check the other rooms."

"I'm way ahead of you, Frank," Joe said as he picked up the screwdriver. At the next shed, he didn't need to use the screwdriver. He could just pull the pins from the hinges. Except for piles of paint-spattered tarps, the room was empty.

After he opened the door to the third shed, he called softly, "Hey, guys, come here!"

Frank and Chet hurried over and saw another man on a cot. Frank recognized him immediately as Jack Parente.

"Thanks a lot, kids," Parente said gratefully as they cut the tape loose from his wrists and ankles.

"You can thank us later," Joe told him, looking around. The funny feeling in the pit of his stomach was growing. It made him nervous that they hadn't come across Goldson or any of the other crooks. "We should get out of here and call the cops. I know Goldson must be planning something. Do you know if Johns is here anywhere?"

"I think he's here somewhere," Parente told him.

Leaving Chet with Kaner and Parente, Frank and Joe went quickly down the row of doors, knocking and listening for sounds. They heard nothing until they came to the last one.

"Anybody inside?" Joe whispered hoarsely as he rapped on the door.

There was an answering rustle of movement, then a long pause. Then Frank and Joe heard a faint voice answer, "It's Barry Johns."

Joe smiled. He was about to work on the hinges when he noticed that the padlock dangled open from the metal loop. Joe pulled the door open.

Barry Johns stood just inside the doorway, dressed in white sweatpants and a green warm-up jacket. He looked tired and drawn, but Joe noticed that, unlike Kaner and Parent, Johns was clean-shaven.

"Who are you?" Johns asked.

"I'm Joe Hardy," Joe replied. "I'm here to help."

"Oh," Johns said softly. He stared nervously at Chet when he appeared a moment later with Kaner and Parente.

Frank was busy checking out Johns's room. It was not a bare little cell like the other two rooms had been. The bed was a comfortable-looking camp bed with a new sleeping bag spread over it.

A five-inch color television and a VCR were perched on a crate at the end of the bed, and an office refrigerator and microwave oven were set up against one wall. There was a pile of microwave dinner wrappers in the corner of the room.

"Well, well, Barry, it looks like you got the kidnappers' deluxe accommodations," Parente quipped, peering into the room. "You always did go first class."

Johns said nothing.

"The creeps didn't even feed me," Kaner complained.

"We'll get you some food as soon as possible," Chet assured him. "Come to think of it, I could use a burger or something myself."

"It'll be burgers all around once we get out of here," Joe said. "And I think Sergeant Hanlon should spring for them. After all, we've just cracked one of the biggest kidnapping cases in San Diego history."

Frank frowned as he continued to glance around Johns's room. Something wasn't right, but there wasn't time to figure it out.

"I wouldn't start patting yourself on the back yet, Joe," Frank warned. "We still have to get out of here. I think Mr. Goldson may have a little surprise for us."

Frank led the silent group toward the shattered door into the factory. He tried to hurry the kidnap victims toward the exit, but Kaner was stiff from his confinement, and he and Johns moved very slowly. Johns didn't seem especially thrilled about being rescued, Frank noted.

As they passed the van, a pair of powerful searchlights suddenly flooded the factory with blinding white light. Unable to see for a minute, the boys froze. They did hear a metal door slide shut with an ominous clang.

Shading his eyes with his hands, Joe peered out and saw their only exit blocked by a locked metal gate. Then his attention was caught by Whip Scorpion's shiny form as he stepped out of the darkness into the light. He flicked his bullwhip with a sharp pop and brandished a ninja star in his other hand. Joe turned again as Flame Fiend appeared on the other side of them, shooting a burst of fire from his hand.

"Now we settle accounts," a gravelly voice announced from behind the boys. "We played you kids just right—like a cat does a mouse. You thought you were getting away, but we watched you the whole time."

The Human Dreadnought was standing on the roof of the van. The boys were surrounded.

Chapter 14

FRANK HAD TAKEN a step back when Flame Fiend and Whip Scorpion emerged from the shadows. His eyes adjusted to the light quickly, and he noticed some equipment piled up on the crates next to him. On top of the pile was a small laser, and it was aimed right at the Human Dreadnought. Without turning his head, Frank caught his brother's eye. Joe was checking out a large circuit breaker on the wall next to him then.

Frank made an almost imperceptible gesture with his chin at the laser beside him. Then he tossed his head in the direction of the circuit breaker. Joe nodded. The brothers were so close that they understood each other without having to say a word.

Joe reached out and yanked down the master switch on the side of the circuit breaker, plunging the factory into darkness. At the same moment Frank shot his hand out and flicked a switch on the side of the laser housing. It hummed to life and spat out a brilliant blue beam of light that hit the Dreadnought right in his visor. He shrieked in pain, ducking out of the laser's beam.

It was sunset by now, and only a few dim rays of light leaked through the cracks on the factory's painted-over windows and skylights.

"Joe, meet me back here after you hide Kaner," Frank whispered. He grabbed Johns and Parente and pulled them off into the blackness deeper inside the warehouse.

It was almost completely dark, but Joe remembered seeing a row of lockers on the far wall. He just hoped it was clear going. If they tripped over anything or made any noise, they were dead. They had to move fast, too, and hide before the lights went back on. Keeping his ears cocked for any sound of pursuit, Joe grabbed Chet and Kaner and carefully made his way across the width of the factory. They reached the lockers, and coming to the nearest one, Joe eased the door open and helped Kaner inside.

"Stay there and don't open the door unless you know it's one of us," Joe whispered. Then he led Chet back to the spot where Frank had told him to rendezvous.

Frank led Johns and Parente toward the far end of the factory, where he remembered seeing a pile of garbage. It would make an excellent hiding place. He picked his way carefully through a labyrinth of tall, rusty machinery. It bothered him that Johns was moving so sluggishly, but Frank pushed him forward.

"Get down under that garbage and keep quiet!" Frank whispered when they reached the spot. He piled black plastic garbage bags over both men. Then he turned and crept back to meet Joe.

"Where's Chet?" Frank asked when he found his brother.

"Right here," Joe whispered back. "I picked up a little weapon."

"What?"

Joe held out a can of spray paint for Frank to touch.

"Let's get under cover before they get the lights back on," Frank whispered.

Just as Frank, Joe, and Chet were arranging some dusty plastic tarps over their prone bodies, the lights went back on. The trio drew in their breath and held it as they heard the heavy footsteps of the Human Dreadnought approaching.

"Okay, now that the lights are on again, I want you to find those kids, pronto," the Dreadnought growled.

"They could be anywhere in this maze of junk," Flame Fiend grumbled.

"We'll find them," said the Human Dreadnought. "And when we do, it'll be adios to the whole bunch."

"What about Johns?" asked Flame Fiend.

"Him, too," the Dreadnought snarled. "The whole thing's gotten too complicated. I say we off the whole bunch, then collect the ransoms and hightail it down to Baja. The cops'll never find us down there. You, Scorpion," the Dreadnought went on, "throw your stars to kill. We don't need any witnesses to complicate things."

"Gotcha," Whip Scorpion replied.

Frank tried to lie as still as possible. Feeling Chet twitching next to him, Frank elbowed him to remind him to stay still. When Chet's twitching became more pronounced, Frank turned his head to see what was wrong. Too late, he realized Chet was about to sneeze.

"*Aaaa-chooo!*"

Frank didn't have any time to think before the tarps covering them were ripped aside and he found himself staring up into the face of the Human Dreadnought.

The Dreadnought made a horrible, muffled laugh inside his dark-visored helmet, then lowered his revolver so it was pointing right at Frank. There was an ominous click as the Dreadnought drew the hammer back.

"No slipups this time, kids." He chuckled. "This is the end of the line."

Chapter 15

FRANK CAUGHT a whiff of gun oil and could see the ugly, blunt tips of the bullets inside the revolver's chambers.

"Well, well, well. What a fine bunch of chickens I've caught here," the Dreadnought said in a mocking voice.

"How are we going to cook these chickens, boys?" he asked Whip Scorpion and Flame Fiend.

"How about we fry them?" Whip Scorpion gave a high-pitched, crazy laugh that made Frank's skin crawl.

The Dreadnought swiveled his head back to laugh, and Joe saw his chance. Without wasting a second, he brought up the can of spray paint and let the Dreadnought have it, covering his visor. Then he caught the other two in the face as Frank dodged out of the way of the Dreadnought's gun and lashed out with a karate kick that sent the huge man tumbling backward.

Joe and Frank and Chet were on their feet and running in an instant.

They sprinted into the dark recesses of the huge factory toward the maze of machinery at the far end of the floor, Flame Fiend and Whip Scorpion moving after them. Moving as silently as possible, Joe, Frank, and Chet wove in and out of the rows of rusty machines that loomed over them. Joe scanned the factory walls for exits as he ran, but all the doors and windows were boarded up. He could hear the Dreadnought's angry voice bellowing behind them, and it sounded to Joe as if they were all getting close.

Joe looked frantically around for a way out.

"Over there!" he heard Frank cry.

Joe turned in the direction Frank was pointing and strained his eyes against the dimness. Finally he spotted a light-colored door against the rear wall of the factory.

"Let's go!" Joe said. He ran for the door, letting out a sigh of relief when he tried it and found it wasn't locked.

Joe had the door open and Chet was through it when Whip Scorpion appeared on top of one of the banks of machinery.

"Boss, they're over here!" he shouted. Joe saw Whip Scorpion reach into his belt.

"Run!" Joe shouted to Frank.

As the brothers raced over the threshold, Joe saw something flash, and a ninja star thudded into the doorframe just above his hand. Joe slammed the door closed, and Frank shoved a heavy broom handle through the inside door handle and rested both ends against the doorframe.

He turned and scanned his surroundings. They were in a storeroom of some kind.

"Check behind you on that shelf, Frank," Joe called.

The butt of a gun was visible, but when Frank grabbed the gun butt and pulled it off the shelf, it turned out to be a strange-looking weapon with a flaring cone-shaped muzzle.

"What's this?" Frank asked, puzzled.

Joe studied the strange weapon for a moment, then said, "Wolfe's inventory mentioned a netgun. Maybe this is it."

"What does it do?" Frank asked.

"It shoots a big net, I guess," Joe said.

"Well, it'll only take out one of them at a time. We need a better weapon than this,"

Frank said, leaning the netgun against the wall by the door.

"Hey, fellas, I think I got something!" Chet called excitedly.

He was standing next to a large machine at the far end of the room. It looked like a huge fan mounted on a pivoting base.

"A wind machine," Joe commented. "So what? You want to blow the kidnappers away, Chet?"

"It could get us out of here, Joe," Chet insisted. "I got the idea from this comic I read. There's a scene where the Human Dreadnought's got some of the Green Cyclone's friends trapped in a box canyon. The Cyclone uses his wind powers to lift them out of danger. Maybe we could use the wind machine to carry us up to that skylight." Chet pointed at a painted-over skylight directly above the little storage shed.

Joe shook his head. "Not a bad idea, Chet, but it wouldn't work. We'd need some kind of wings to provide the lift."

Frank snapped his fingers. "Wait a minute! Maybe we could make some 'wings.' "

He went over to a pile of light canvas drop cloths and began cutting them into six-foot squares with his pocketknife. When he'd cut three squares, he looked over at Chet and Joe. "Well, what are you two waiting for? Let's get flying."

"What do we do first?" Chet asked.

Wham! There was a terrific impact on the storeroom door as the Human Dreadnought hurled himself against it. The thick broom handle held, but the Dreadnought hurled himself against the door again and again.

"We'd better get this show on the road," Joe said, taking one of the pieces of cloth from Frank.

Joe finished tying the square of cloth around his wrists and ankles while Frank and Chet moved the fan into position below the skylight.

The kidnappers hurled themselves against the door with redoubled fury, and Joe heard the handle begin to splinter.

"I'm ready!" Joe said, clambering up on the makeshift platform Chet had thrown together from some packing boxes. "Is that wind machine ready?"

Frank flicked a switch, and the wind machine's huge blades began turning, quickly increasing in speed.

Joe tensed, then jumped with his arms and legs spread wide. He half-expected to crash down onto the fan, but to his astonishment he felt himself rising toward the skylight.

Joe was soon high enough to grab a piece of a thin metal support framing the skylight.

"Okay!" he shouted as the kidnappers threw themselves against the door again.

Joe watched as Chet climbed up on the pile of boxes. Chet glanced up at him nervously, then leapt with his arms and legs wide. He hung suspended in midair for a long moment, then began to rise, although more slowly than Joe had.

Joe tracked Chet's rise until he was close enough to reach. Grabbing a metal support and bracing his feet, Joe held out his hand to Chet, who grabbed it. Joe pulled his friend close enough so that Chet, who was white-faced and sweating, could grab another support with his free hand and clamber up into the support struts.

Looking down, Joe saw that Frank had strapped the netgun across his chest. Then he heard the Dreadnought discharge his revolver into the supply-room door. The big handgun crashed twice in a row, splintering the wooden handle that had been holding it shut.

Looking over his shoulder at the door, Frank clambered up onto the crates and leapt, letting himself be carried upward on the column of air.

Before Frank had risen high enough for Joe to reach him, the Dreadnought slammed into the door again. This time the door swung open.

Taking one look at Frank, the Dreadnought strode over to the wind machine and popped off the protective grille that covered the blade. Joe watched in horror as the Dreadnought shut off the machine.

"Frank!" Joe reached out for his brother's hand and felt their fingertips brush for a second.

Then Frank began to sink toward the naked blades of the wind machine, which were still slowly turning.

Chapter 16

FRANK FELT HIMSELF falling. Then, a split second later, Joe's hand snaked down with lightning speed and grabbed Frank's wrist. He felt a strong jolt in his shoulder, but somehow he managed to clamber up beside Joe and Chet in the supports. Flame Fiend fired a bolt of flame up at them, but it fell short.

"Quick! Let's get out of here!" Joe exclaimed.

The boys hurried over to the skylight and boosted themselves through it to the catwalk that ran along the outside of the roof.

There's a ladder there," Joe said, pointing as he, Frank, and Chet got rid of their wings.

"We'll have to split up," Frank said. "Chet, you get the cops. Joe and I'll find a way to hang the kidnappers up till the cops come."

"The catwalk goes all the way around the building, Chet," Joe told him. "Go around to the other side. There's probably another ladder. Find a phone and get the cops here. Got it?"

Chet answered with a thumbs-up sign, then hurried along the catwalk as Joe and Frank headed for the near ladder.

As they reached the ladder, Frank heard someone scrambling up it. He spotted a pair of short smokestacks jutting up from the roof above the factory entrance. He and Joe flung themselves behind the stacks, and Frank kept the netgun trained on the ladder.

Soon he heard the soft clanging sounds of someone climbing the ladder much closer. A moment later Lenny Goldson's face appeared over the top. He had taken off his helmet, but was still wearing the rest of his Human Dreadnought costume.

When Goldson reached the top of the ladder, Joe shouted, "Now, Frank!'

The netgun made a whooshing pop sound as it fired, and the net expanded instantly, carrying Goldson backward off the ladder.

Frank heard Goldson hit the ground with a meaty thud. "Come on, Joe, let's make sure Goldson's out!" he called over his shoulder as he ran over to the ladder.

Frank and Joe saw that Goldson was wrapped in the net, unconscious at the bottom of the ladder.

"You knocked him out colder than a mackerel," Joe said with a grin.

"Don't waste any time patting me on the

back, Joe," Frank said. "We still have to catch the other two kidnappers."

Frank and Joe sneaked back through the skylight. Silently they dropped onto a pile of empty cardboard boxes. On the other side of the factory they heard a commotion.

"Hey," Frank whispered to Joe, "that sounds like it's coming from where I left Johns and Parente."

"Let's get over there!" Joe said, racing out the door.

They slowed to a crawl as they came up behind a row of machines. From there they could see that Flame Fiend was holding his flamethrower on Johns and Parente, while Whip Scorpion was guarding Syd Kaner.

Frank reached into his shoulder bag, pulled out his tape recorder, and silently switched it on. ". . . can still collect the ransom for Parente," he heard Johns say.

"I don't know," Flame Fiend responded dubiously.

Johns took a step toward Flame Fiend, saying, "Parente's ransom is the only money you'll have for a getaway."

Whip Scorpion's masked head bobbed up and down as he nodded. "Yeah. That makes sense."

Flame Fiend and Whip Scorpion grabbed Parente and Kaner and dragged them off, with Johns nervously trailing behind.

Joe shot Frank a surprised look, and Frank

whispered, "Johns is in on it, too, Joe. Every time I thought about it, that was the only thing that made sense. Now I know for sure."

"What now?" Joe asked.

"Let's shadow them and wait for an opening. If we rush them, Parente and Kaner might get hurt."

The Hardys had gone only a few yards when the sound of sirens cut the air. Joe saw headlights shine into the factory, silhouetting Flame Fiend, Johns, and Parente where they stood.

Two black-and-white San Diego P.D. cars pulled up in front of the factory entrance, and four uniformed officers piled out of the cars, led by a huge black man wearing a rumpled suit. Frank recognized Sergeant Hanlon immediately.

"Police! Freeze!" Hanlon barked.

"Whew!" Frank let out a sigh of relief as Flame Fiend and Whip Scorpion raised their hands. "I never thought I'd be so glad to see Hanlon's ugly face."

"Me, either," Joe agreed.

"Don't shoot, Hanlon," Joe announced as he and Frank came out from behind the machinery. "It's the Hardys."

Hanlon looked at them and waved for them to come over. As Frank and Joe approached, Hanlon stuck out a hand. "Good work, Frank, Joe."

"Thanks, Sergeant," Frank said, "but don't you think your men should put cuffs on the gang's leader, Barry Johns?"

Johns's face grew pale. "That's absurd! I'm just an innocent victim!" he sputtered.

"Oh, really?" Frank answered sarcastically. He pulled his mini tape recorder from his shoulder bag, rewound the tape, and played back the fragments of Johns's conversation with Flame Fiend.

Johns's face went even whiter, but he remained indignant. "That doesn't prove anything! Who are you going to listen to, Sergeant, me or a couple of kids?"

"Wait, there's more," Frank announced. He told Hanlon about Morrie Rockwitz's purchase of Johns's art collection.

"Did you have the police lab analyze the age of that page fragment Frank gave you?" Joe asked.

"Sure," Hanlon responded. "The lab boys said it was only a few years old."

"Then it's a fake," Chet said. "A real Golden Age page would be forty or fifty years old."

"We know that Johns had been selling off his collection for years, whenever he needed money," Frank said. "He replaced the originals with forgeries. Johns wanted to collect on the insurance policy for his collection, so he had himself kidnapped and arranged for the forgeries to be burned during the kidnapping."

"Okay, I've heard enough," Hanlon said. Turning to one of the other officers, he instructed, "Put the cuffs on Johns, Willy."

* * *

An hour and a half later Joe, Frank, Chet, Parente, and Kaner sat in Hanlon's office making their statements.

"You'll have to ask Johns about this, but our theory is that he had several reasons for grabbing his staff. For one thing, Johns was greedy. He wanted the ransoms to add to his take from the insurance," Joe said.

"For another thing," he continued, "Johns was really vain. He wanted people to think he'd been doing all the work on his company's titles, even though Parente and Kaner were doing most of it. He hoped to shut them up permanently and also to stop the lawsuit they were bringing against him."

"That's true!" Jack Parente said emphatically. "Me and Syd here were both suing to get out of our contracts and to recover the royalties he was cheating us out of."

"Yeah," Kaner agreed. "For years Barry had us ghosting stuff that he signed his name to. We both got sick of it."

"What about Harry Saul?" Frank asked.

"Harry was helping us sue Johns," Parente explained. "He hates Barry so much he'd do anything to get back at him."

"It's just coincidence that you saw Harry pass my house the day of the kidnapping. He was coming over to drop off some papers from our lawyer," Kaner put in.

"But why was Saul with Rockwitz?" Joe asked in a puzzled tone.

"I can explain that," Chet answered. "Just before we came in here, I called Tom. He told me he'd tracked down Rockwitz. Rockwitz said Saul wanted one of the pieces from Johns's collection. A cover of a Golden Age comic Saul had published. Rockwitz wouldn't sell it because it was evidence, so Saul threatened him."

"How about blowing up Zenith's office?" Hanlon asked. "Was that just for the insurance?"

"Yes," Frank answered, "and to cover the theft of any equipment from the Zenith offices that Johns used in the kidnappings, like the computer and printer we found. Besides, the bombing made it look like there was a vendetta against Johns and his company."

"That fits." Hanlon nodded. "And the kidnapping attempt on Dewey Strong was supposed to look like part of the vendetta, too, huh?"

"Partially," Joe put in. "But Johns might also have been afraid that Strong might confess to stealing Metaman and give Saul a chance to reopen his plagiarism suit."

"But why go to all the trouble of having the kidnappers fake superpowers?" Hanlon asked.

"Johns had them dress like Terrific Comics characters to cast suspicion on Harry Saul," Frank said. "The supervillains got into their parts so much that they couldn't even attack us in the warehouse without changing into their outfits."

"Johns may have been greedy," Joe observed, "but he was shrewd, too. He faked being a prisoner so he'd have a perfect alibi. He was a prisoner while the crimes were being committed. And if the scheme worked, he would have enough money from the ransoms and the insurance to pay off his debts and start another company."

"What about Mrs. Johns? Was she in on it, too?" Chet asked.

Hanlon said she'd been taken in by her husband, too. "Got somewhere you need to be?" he asked Chet after Chet had checked his watch for the fourth time.

Chet looked at him eagerly. "Well, I was kind of hoping we'd get out of here in time to catch the dance at the comic con. Seduction of the Innocent is playing—that's a band that's made up of all writers and artists from the comics business."

Hanlon flipped his notebook closed. "I guess we're done with all of you. You just might make your dance."

"I'll go with you, Chet," Joe volunteered. "After three days of nothing but chasing crooks, I'm ready for a little fun!"

"You can count me in, too!" Frank said.

The next morning Frank, Joe, and Chet lay in the sun at Ocean Beach. Chet was stretched out on his Metaman beach towel, with his white beach hat pulled down over his eyes, snoring loudly.

"All that sleep he missed during the con must have caught up with him," Frank said to Joe.

When Joe didn't answer, Frank looked past Chet to where Joe's towel was and did a double-take. Instead of watching the many bikini-clad lovelies all around him, as Frank expected his brother would be doing, Joe was intently reading an issue of the *Green Cyclone*.

"Say, Joe," Frank called with a grin. "Are you studying to become a superhero?"

"Nope," he replied, "but after Chet saved us with a trick from a comic book, I figured I'd better bone up on my comics for our next case!"

Frank and Joe's next case:

While attending an international summer school at England's Oxford University, the Hardys learn just how much times have changed. Frank's roommate, Pyotr Zigonev, is the USSR junior chess champ, and he has become a pawn in an international power play. But just as the boys rally to Zigonev, they discover that the CIA has joined forces with the KGB!

The American and Soviet spy masters are out to foil a master of terrorism, and Frank, Joe, and Zigonev are caught in the middle. One false move and they'll lose the ultimate game—a danger-packed contest played out in the cold gray shadows of Stonehenge . . . in *Strategic Moves*, Case #43 in The Hardy Boys Casefiles™.